CAST OF CHARACTERS

FAMILY
SECRETS

*Five extraordinary siblings. One dangerous past.
Unlimited potential.*

Jack Ingram—To save his brother's life, he sacrificed himself to the Coalition. But one woman could end this deadly game for good and set his aching heart free.

Mariah Daley—The undercover FBI agent was assigned to protect Jake from the Coalition, but could she convince him to trust her with his life…and his love?

Agnes Payne and Oliver Grimble—Their evildoing divided a family of superchildren, only to bring the genius siblings together years later as a stronger, united front that now threatens to destroy the Coalition once and for all.

General Bruno DeBruzkya—Seeing the Coalition about to crumble, the power-hungry dictator is out to find a new path to conquer the world.

About the Author

BEVERLY BARTON

is the award-winning, bestselling author of over fifty books. She's been in love with romance since her grandfather gave her an illustrated copy of *Beauty and the Beast*. An avid reader since childhood, she wrote her first book at the age of nine. After over thirty-five years of marriage to the love of her life, Beverly is a true romantic and considers writing romance novels a real labor of love.

When asked to participate in the FAMILY SECRETS continuity series, Beverly couldn't resist when told her hero, Jake Ingram, was a man who possessed superpowers. Intrigued by the innovative idea of Jake and his siblings being the products of genetic engineering, she looked forward to conquering the most difficult part of writing a continuity series— finding a way to make the characters truly belong to the author. Readers were introduced to Jake early on in the series, so Beverly understood that reader expectation would be very high by the time they read Jake's book. She envisioned him as "the man," the to-die-for hero. So with a hero this strong and ultramacho, it was only natural to give him a heroine who was his equal in every way, which Mariah is— and then some.

BEVERLY
BARTON

CHECK
MATE

literaryleftovers@juno.com

813 W Main St. #103
Battle Ground, WA 98604

Published by Silhouette Books
America's Publisher of Contemporary Romance

Special thanks and acknowledgment are given to Beverly Barton for her contribution to the FAMILY SECRETS series.

SILHOUETTE BOOKS

ISBN 0-373-61379-2

CHECK MATE

Visit Silhouette at www.eHarlequin.com

Printed in U.S.A.

FAMILY SECRETS

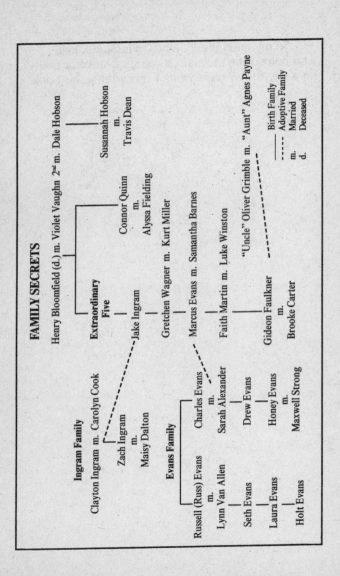

Henry Bloomfield (d.) m. Violet Vaughn 2nd m. Dale Hobson

Susannah Hobson
m.
Travis Dean

Ingram Family

Clayton Ingram m. Carolyn Cook

Extraordinary Five

Jake Ingram

Zach Ingram
m.
Maisy Dalton

Connor Quinn
m.
Alyssa Fielding

Gretchen Wagner m. Kurt Miller

Marcus Evans m. Samantha Barnes

Faith Martin m. Luke Winston

Gideon Faulkner
m.
Brooke Carter

"Uncle" Oliver Grimble m. "Aunt" Agnes Payne

Evans Family

Russell (Russ) Evans
m.
Lynn Van Allen

Charles Evans
m.
Sarah Alexander

Seth Evans

Drew Evans

Laura Evans

Honey Evans
m.
Maxwell Strong

Holt Evans

Birth Family
Adoptive Family
m.   Married
d.   Deceased

To my good friend, Linda Winstead Jones,
who helped me maintain some semblance of sanity
on a day-to-day basis while I was writing this book.

Prologue

"'There was a crooked man, who walked a crooked mile...'" As the phrase played over and over in Gideon Faulkner's mind, shattering the final block on his memory of childhood, Jake Ingram took advantage of the situation.

I love you, Bro, Jake thought as he socked Gideon, landing a perfect hit and sending his brother careening to the ground. Immediately Jake headed down the path toward the secret entrance to the underground compound high in the Oregon mountains. He would do what Gideon had planned to do—retrieve the computer disk containing evidence against the Coalition and destroy all the work Gideon had started on the next Coalition crime. Equally important was gaining access to another disk that would simultaneously cut off the Coalition accounts.

Jake knew one thing for certain—he had to get inside the compound before his brother regained consciousness and came after him. Jake had weighed the odds, then done what was necessary. He'd known the risks involved. But what else could he have done? No way in hell was he going to allow his brother to put his life on the line, not after all Gideon had been through since childhood as the pawn of manipulative, self-serving monsters. Especially not now that Gideon had found someone to love, Brooke Carter. Gideon deserved a real life, with a woman who loved him, a woman willing to accept him for who and what he was.

Becoming the big brother to five adult siblings had come as a surprise to Jake, and to those sisters and brothers he'd been brainwashed to forget ever existed. But his newfound family meant everything to him and he intended to do whatever was necessary to protect them. And the one way to keep all those he loved safe was to bring down the Coalition and to make sure the new Code Proteus experiments were confiscated. Jake and his siblings knew better than anyone the devastating results of the original experiments. Their own biological father, a brilliant scientist, had spearheaded the original Code Proteus project of genetic engineering. Henry Bloomfield had imagined designing babies with the physical abilities of superheroes, the intellect of geniuses, the creative and leadership abilities of the world's greatest philosophers and political leaders.

Six children had been born—Henry's own biological offspring—in two different births, three children each. Jake had been the firstborn of the first set of triplets, but at age twelve, all memory of his parents and his birthright had been wiped from his mind. Then less than a year ago, he had learned the truth about his past when his biological mother, Violet, had finally found him and made contact. After that, Jake had begun an extensive search for his siblings and located them, one by one. But before they had the chance to get to know their mother again, she'd been murdered by the people who had used Gideon for their evil purposes.

Although Jake had been raised with a brother—the son of the wonderful family that had adopted him when he was twelve—he felt a deep, inexplicable connection to his biological siblings, who shared with him not only the same parents, but were, as he was, the products of genetically engineered human embryos being implanted into a surrogate female. He was one of the genetically enhanced superkids, one of the Extraordinary Five.

Following the directions Gideon had shared with him about where the secret entrance to the underground compound was located, Jake made his way through the dense forest. The January wind seeped through his heavy winter coat and fleece-lined leather gloves, as his boots crunched over snow-covered, rotting vegetation. He kept the flashlight beam pointing downward, illuminating the path before him without giving away his location. Towering age-old trees, with barren limbs creaking in the frigid wind, surrounded him, like dark giants watching his every move. With dawn fast approaching, he didn't have long to make it to the destination and get inside the compound without alerting the guards to his presence.

He was close. So close. Hurry. Walk faster. Run. A voice inside his head shouted instructions. Suddenly, from out of nowhere, six black-clad figures appeared, boxing him in, blocking his path. Damn! He couldn't run; there was no escape. And it was highly unlikely that he could overpower six men, all probably military trained. So, what are you going to do? Jake asked himself. He'd never been one to give up, no matter what the odds against him. The way he saw it, there was only one thing to do—put up the fight of his life. And thank God he was the one the Coalition had captured and not Gideon.

One

Emerging from a groggy, drug-induced fog, Jake Ingram fought to clear his mind. Where was he? What had happened? What was going on? He tried to open his eyes, but found the effort too exhausting. Damn it, man, try again. What the hell's the matter with you?

Could be he was asleep and having a nightmare. Yeah, maybe that was it. Try to wake up, he told himself. He did his best to move, to shake his head, lift his arm—do anything that might bring him around—but to no avail.

"I think our guest is coming to," someone said, but Jake didn't recognize the voice.

"Yeah, well, it's about time," a deeper, grittier voice responded.

"Should I give him another shot?"

"Nah, we'll be there soon and it'll be easier for us to get him inside the cabin if he's able to walk. I don't want to have to carry him. He's a damn big man."

"Yeah, you got that right. And strong as an ox. Brinker told me he fought like a tiger when they surrounded him. The guy's got grit to take on six men.''

''You'd better check his cuffs. He may be a bit fuzzy when he gets good and awake, but he could still try to give us some trouble.''

Jake felt someone's hands on him—quick, rough hands that slid behind his back to grip his wrists, then reached down and grasped each ankle in turn. What was the guy doing? Checking your cuffs, Jake reminded himself of what he'd heard the two men discussing. Cuffs? Did they have him handcuffed?

''He's secure, but he'll have a hell of a time walking with those leg irons on.''

''I'm not setting him loose until the doc takes a look at him and starts doing her hoodoo thing,'' the deep voice said. ''Our orders are to keep him confined for her. We can rough him up, but we aren't supposed to kill him. Unless, of course, he gives us a good reason to.''

Loud, robust laughter echoed inside Jake's head. He wanted to tell the men to stop laughing, stop talking about him as if he weren't there, but he couldn't manage to get his mouth open wide enough to speak.

Who were these men? Where were they taking him? Why did they have his wrists and ankles cuffed? What's the last thing you remember? Jake asked himself.

He'd been with Gideon, trying to talk him out of entering the underground compound in Oregon to retrieve the computer disk where he'd stored information that could destroy the Coalition. But he hadn't been able to talk sense to his brother, so he'd…God, he'd coldcocked him! Then he'd hurried along the path toward the compound's secret entrance. He had been close—so close.

Jake raked his tongue around inside his mouth, then licked his lips. The metallic taste of blood—dried blood—registered in his mind. He'd been hit in the face, punched in the mouth. A nagging ache in his ribs reminded him that he'd put up a good fight, but he'd lost. Now he remembered. Six black-clad goons had surrounded him. He'd been captured before entering the compound. Undoubtedly they'd drugged him for transport. But where was he?

As the feeling returned to his body and his mind registered the things his five senses picked up, he realized he was moving, that he was inside a vehicle of some sort. His eyelids quivered. That's it, he told himself. Open your eyes and take a good look. Whatever is happening, you'll have to find a logical way to deal with it. He knew his life depended on how well he handled the situation. His heavy eyelids opened lazily. It took a good minute or two for his eyesight to adjust to the shadowy interior of the SUV. Looking straight ahead, he saw the back of two heads—one with scraggy brown hair that touched the collar of his blue plaid coat and one with military-short blond hair. As best Jake could make out, the broad-shouldered blonde, who wore a tan suede jacket, was driving what appeared to be a fairly new four-wheel drive. Jake pegged him to be the gruff-spoken one of the two. The second guy, who had a smaller build and fidgeted nervously, was fumbling with the radio, scanning for a station.

"Might as well forget it," the driver said. "You're not getting anything but static."

Shaggy-hair grumbled. "This assignment is the pits. You know, Burgess, being holed up in a cabin in the frozen hills of Arizona guarding a genius freak isn't my idea of a good time. I'll go bonkers after a few days. You've heard of cabin fever, haven't you? Well, I got it and we aren't even at the cabin, yet."

"Quit bellyaching," Burgess said. "Les, you're as whiny as an old woman. We're doing what we've been told to do, what we're getting paid to do. Besides, it might not take the doc that long to get inside pretty boy's head."

Les chuckled. "He's not all that pretty with his busted lip and bruised face." When Les glanced into the back seat, Jake closed his eyes. "So this guy is one of those superhumans, huh? He looks pretty ordinary to me."

"Well, don't let his looks fool you. I was told the guy's a financial whiz, a real mathematical genius. Seems he's the big dog of the litter. And the Coalition wants him working on their side. That's why the doc is waiting on us. It's her job to reactivate him."

"Reactivate him?"

Les finally found a radio station, although the reception wasn't great. A Sixties rock hit blasted from the radio and reverberated inside the SUV.

"Turn that damn thing down." Burgess gave his partner a sharp glance, which prompted him to lower the volume. "It seems those superkids, the Extraordinary Five, were put through some sort of hypnotic conditioning when they were children so that they could be controlled. The boss wants this guy reconditioned."

"What do you know about Doc? I don't even know her name. Is she a real doc or just a shrink?"

"She's a psychiatrist. Her name's Dr. Brooks. We're suppose to follow her orders. I was told that she'd be in charge."

"I don't like taking orders from a woman."

While Les and Burgess went back and forth on the advantages versus the disadvantages of having a female boss, Jake took the opportunity to look out the windows and see if he could pick up any visual details that might help him. All he knew—from what Les had said—was that they were in Arizona. The more he knew about his location, about the surrounding territory, the better prepared he'd be when he made his escape. And he would escape. Somehow. Someway.

Jake wondered if it was later the same day—the same day he'd been ambushed. If so, then he would have been flown from Oregon to Arizona. But if it was the following day, while it was possible that Les and Burgess had driven the entire distance overnight,

Jake would lay odds that he'd been flown to some private airstrip, then picked up by these two thugs.

When he surveyed the area outside the SUV, what he saw didn't surprise him, but it did frustrate him. They were headed up a mountainside, driving through rough terrain, although the road appeared to be paved. Golden rabbitbrush and a fresh layer of snow covered the ground, and in the distance he saw snow-coated, barren rock formations. His captors kept talking about a cabin—no doubt some isolated retreat that belonged to the Coalition—and about a woman doctor—a psychiatrist they'd called Dr. Brooks.

The Coalition wanted to reactivate his programing, done when he'd been a boy by Oliver Grimble and Agnes Payne, two of his father's colleagues, who had secretly implanted psychological messages—phrase triggers—in his young mind to make him easier to control. But he hadn't been the only one whose mind had been tampered with by the gruesome couple. Each one of the Extraordinary Five had suffered the same fate.

Suddenly the vehicle lurched and bounced, tossing them about despite the restraint of their seat belts. Jake realized they had left the paved road and were traveling over a rocky, rutted trail leading higher into the mountains. Burgess dropped into four-wheel drive and they continued at a snail's pace. Snow-laden junipers, pines and chaparral lined the narrow roadway, and although the vehicle's heater seemed to be working just fine, Jake felt a sudden chill and realized the temperature was dropping quickly as the sun was setting. The rugged dirt road wound about in a series of steep switchbacks up the mountainside, taking them higher and higher, deeper and deeper into the godforsaken wilderness.

If he tried to get away—and he intended to—he would face several major obstacles. First and foremost, his hands and feet were shackled. But they wouldn't keep him bound once the good doctor started her treatments. The first problem would be solved then. The second handicap was his location. He didn't know the area, and traveling on foot in these dangerous hills in a January winter would be deadly. He'd just have to find a way to secure a vehicle—either this SUV or the doctor's car. Second problem solved. The third obstacle would be escaping from Les and Burgess. Both men were probably well-armed, so it would take some real finagling to get past them. He'd just have to find a way to disarm them and render them harmless. A problem yet to be solved.

And what about Dr. Brooks? Jake asked himself. Hell, she was only a woman. Managing her should be the easiest part of the great escape.

As his two captors continued conversing, Jake picked up snippets of their conversation, most totally irrelevant to his current situation. One rock song after another added background music to the jabbering, and except for an occasional glimpse into the back seat, neither man paid much attention to Jake. He studied the landscape, trying to find some sort of marker that might let him know he was on the right path when he made the return trip alone after his escape, but everything was beginning to look the same. Then suddenly he noticed a stream bed. Cold, white water and frozen slush cascaded down a series of large brown boulders, creating a miniature waterfall. This was definitely something worth remembering.

Creeping along the winding road, they soon became embraced by thick wooded areas on either side, shutting them off from everything except the dying embers of sunlight as twilight approached. Jake tested his handcuffs and leg irons. Totally secure. No room to maneuver. And even though he was thinking straight and his five senses were working properly, he wasn't sure how much physical strength he had left, after having tried to fight off six attackers and being drugged for God only knew how many hours.

While he was considering his options and surmising that at present he had only one—cooperation—a midsize log house appeared in the distance. The sunset melted into the treetops at the back of the cabin, so Jake knew the place faced east. The structure was modern, practically brand-new from the looks of it. Had the Coalition moved their headquarters? Jake wondered. Was this part of a new compound?

"Well, at least the place isn't a dump," Les said. "How many bedrooms? If there's not enough to go around, I'd be happy to share with Doc. Unless she turns out to be a real hag.''

Burgess chuckled. ''I hear she's not bad to look at. But you keep your hands off her or you'll be in big trouble. And I'm told she carries a gun. If you get too friendly, she just might shoot you.''

''What if she won't keep her hands off me?''

''You wish.''

When Burgess drove up to the two-car attached garage, the door opened immediately, which to Jake meant that someone—the lady doctor?—had been waiting and watching. Once the SUV was encased inside the garage, beside a late model Chevy TrailBlazer, the door closed, sealing them inside. Snapping their seat belts loose, Burgess and Les jumped out of the vehicle, then Burgess rounded the hood and came around to Jake's side. Les opened the door and looked Jake over from head to toe. Jake feigned grogginess, letting his eyelids open and close languidly.

Les reached out and shook him. ''Wake up, Ingram. We're not going to carry you.''

Jake opened his eyes and stared into Les's leathery tan face. He figured this guy was close to forty. ''Where am I?'' Jake asked, making his voice sound weak.

''You're where nobody can find you,'' Les replied. ''Now come on and get out.'' He grabbed Jake's arm and urged him to move.

Jake turned and slid off the seat, letting his feet

hit the concrete garage floor. With his legs bound, he found it difficult to balance his body's weight properly and teetered back and forth precariously. Burgess clamped his meaty hand down on Jake's shoulder.

"Get behind him," Burgess told Les, then said to Jake, "You follow me. Take your time or you'll fall flat on your face and I'm not going to pick you up. Got it?"

Jake nodded, then as soon as Les took up his rearguard position, Burgess headed toward the closed door that led into the house. With no choice but to move slowly, Jake hobbled behind Burgess. Once or twice, Les punched him in the back, apparently aggravated the simple task was taking so long.

Burgess grasped the doorknob and the door swung open. Jake followed the young blond ruffian inside, directly into a large living room and dining room combination. The furniture, though inexpensive, appeared to be as new as the cabin.

"So where is she?" Les asked.

Jake was wondering the same thing. If there was a Coalition psychiatrist waiting to start experimenting on his mind, then where the hell was she?

"Dr. Brooks?" Burgess called out in his deep, gravelly voice. "Hey, it's Burgess and Lester. We've got Jake Ingram with us."

Footsteps tapped on the wooden stairs that led to the upper floor. Within minutes, a pair of long, slender legs encased in denim jeans appeared. All three men stared upward to get a good look at the doctor. As unexpected as waking to find that he'd been drugged and was being held captive, Jake's reaction to the woman was even more unexpected. And completely unanticipated. Jake Ingram felt as if he'd been poleaxed, a condition completely unknown to him until this very minute.

Tall—really tall—probably somewhere around five-ten, the lady had the figure of a runway model, one who worked out regularly. Thin, athletic, every inch toned to perfection. Legs that went on forever, slim hips and enough bosom to fill out her bulky turtleneck sweater nicely. But it wasn't her figure alone that staggered Jake. There was something about the whole package that aroused him. Damn, was he crazy? This bitch worked for the Coalition. She was the enemy. Yeah, sure. His brain knew it, but tell that to his body.

Jake couldn't take his eyes off her as she entered the living room. Her long, wavy, jet-black hair had been confined in a loose ponytail and pulled away from her broad face. As his gaze moved down her body again, he noticed the hip holster she wore. The lady was armed—and definitely dangerous.

"There's no need to shout," she said, her voice commanding, yet utterly feminine. "You're...?" She looked directly at the burly blond.

"Burgess, ma'am."

She glanced at the smaller man. "And by process of elimination, you must be Lester." Her gaze moved on to Jake. She did a quick double take, as if seeing him had somehow shocked her. Jake couldn't help wondering if he affected her the way she did him. "And you must be Jake Ingram." She studied his cuffed hands and manacled ankles.

As her azure-blue eyes inspected him thoroughly, her gaze softened ever so slightly, as if she felt a modicum of compassion. When her gaze lifted and met Jake's, he almost grinned, but he wasn't sure whether the humor came from realizing this sultry brunette was sizing him up or from the lunacy of the whole idea that they'd been instantly attracted to each other. Suddenly she frowned and glanced away. Jake noted that her nose was long and straight, her lips wide and full. She wore only a minimum of makeup and a clear gloss on her naturally rosy lips.

Les socked Jake in the side. "When the doc asks you a question, answer her."

Jake winced. Damn but his ribs were sore. "Yes, I'm Jake Ingram. And that's all the information I'll offer you."

"Smart mouth!" Les punched him in the ribs again.

Jake hunched his shoulders and snarled as he glowered at Les.

"That's quite enough," Dr. Brooks said. "Please, undo his leg irons and give me the key to his handcuffs." She held out her open palm.

"I'm not sure that's a good idea," Burgess said.

"This guy could easily overpower you. Take a good look at him, Doc. He's a pretty big fellow."

"I've downed bigger men," she replied, without missing a beat. "I'm thoroughly trained to handle uncooperative patients."

Burgess retrieved a key from his pants pocket, knelt down and unlocked Jake's leg irons, then he stood and tossed the doctor another set of keys. "I'd keep those handcuffs on him if I were you."

"I intend to," she said as she pocketed the keys. "At least for the time being. But I've prepared a room upstairs for our patient, and it will be easier for him to climb the steps without those." She eyed the discarded restraints.

"Why upstairs?" Burgess looked toward the back of the house where two doors stood open.

"I thought it best to confine him upstairs," Dr. Brooks explained. "Less chance of escape. And more privacy for my sessions with him. Besides, there are twin beds in the room upstairs and I plan to be with Mr. Ingram most of the time, so I'll share a room with him."

"You might want to rethink that one, Doc," Les said. "He might get fresh with you." Les chuckled, but shut up instantly when Dr. Brooks gave him a withering glare.

"I assure you, Lester, that I'm more than capable of protecting myself against unwanted attention from Mr. Ingram…or from anyone else."

"Guess she told you." Burgess grinned at Les,

then asked the doctor, "You need any help getting him upstairs?"

"No, thank you. I believe I can handle things… even if he's uncooperative." She glanced meaningfully at her hip holster.

Jake resisted the urge to bend down and rub his ankles. Instead he stood tall and straight, his gaze fixed on Dr. Brooks. He realized that not only couldn't he trust this woman, but he couldn't trust his own feelings about her. The fact that he found her sexually attractive could put him at a disadvantage, but only if he allowed the chemistry between them to distract him from his objective—escape.

"Mr. Ingram, please go out into the hall and up the stairs," Dr. Brooks said. "I'll be right behind you. And if you're thinking of doing something foolish, I'd advise against it."

Jake nodded, then without responding verbally, turned and headed toward the hall. With each step, he subtly studied the house. Knowledge was power. The more he knew about everything that affected him here in this isolated log cabin, the better his chances of finding an opportunity to escape. As he made his way up the wooden stairs, he felt her behind him and heard her footsteps echoing his own. When he reached the top of the stairs, he was facing the bathroom, the door ajar enough to reveal a compact area consisting of a tub/shower combination, a white freestanding sink and an economical white commode.

"Our room is to your left," she told him.

He turned and walked into the 14' x 12' room. Wooden floors and walls. Two windows, one over each of the twin beds, each covered with wooden blinds. Sliding doors that he assumed hid a large closet. A wooden desk with a chair against one wall and a large, overstuffed chair in the opposite corner. Nothing fancy by anyone's standards, but clean and orderly.

"At night, I'll handcuff you to the bedpost," she told him. "I regret doing it, but it will be necessary. At all other times, your cuffs will be removed…as long as you behave yourself. Do you understand?"

"I believe so."

"Turn around, please."

He did. She took the keys from her pocket and unlocked his handcuffs, then removed them and tossed them on the bed to her left. "Would you like to use the bathroom?"

"A shower and a shave would be nice." He rubbed the beard stubble on his chin and cheeks.

"I see no problem with that. There's everything you'll need in the bathroom." She walked across the room, slid open the closet door and retrieved a terrycloth robe. "Leave your jacket on the bed and take this—" she tossed the robe, which he caught midair "—and go to the bathroom. After you've undressed, toss your things out into the hall and I'll take them downstairs to the laundry room."

"Service with a smile," he said. "Who could ask for anything more?"

She glared at him.

"Well, maybe not with a smile," he amended.

"If you're thinking of trying to get out one of the windows, forget it," she told him. "There are bars on both windows in the bedroom and the one in the bathroom."

"You people think of everything."

"We try."

Jake laid the robe on the bed, then removed his jacket and exchanged it for the robe, which he tossed over his shoulder. Dr. Brooks watched him closely as he walked out of the room, into the hall and straight to the bathroom door.

He glanced over his shoulder. "Coming in with me?"

"You seem awfully glib for a man in your situation." She narrowed her gaze speculatively. "You do realize your life is in danger, don't you? Unless you do exactly as you're told and cooperate fully—"

"Tell me, Doc, how did a woman like you get involved with the Coalition?"

"You don't know what kind of woman I am, Mr. Ingram."

"You're right, I don't. But if I'm here for a few days, I might get a chance to find out."

When she didn't refute his comment, he studied her expression. There it was again—that hint of compassion in her eyes. Or was he imagining it, simply seeing what he wanted to see?

Jake went into the bathroom, closed the door and stripped completely, then cracked open the door. "Here they are." He poked the clothes through the opening.

When Dr. Brooks reached out to take the clothes from him, he grasped her wrist. She tensed, but made no move to retreat or attack. Their gazes held and locked.

"Let go," she told him. "I really don't want to resort to violence, but I will, if necessary."

He released her immediately. She took the clothes, turned and headed for the stairs.

"Hey, Doc."

She halted, but didn't turn around. "Yes?"

"You should know that I bend, but don't break. Whatever little mind games you have in store for me—they aren't going to work."

"I guess we'll see, won't we, Jake?"

So that was how she intended to play this. Like a chess match. Each step of the way, seeing who could outsmart and outmaneuver the other. He could probably handle Burgess and Lester. But this woman posed a real problem. Whoever she was and for whatever reason she was working for the Coalition, she was no mere flunky.

"Yeah, I guess we'll see," he said. "By the way, if you get to call me Jake, then what should I call you?"

"Dr. Brooks."

He shook his head. "What's your given name?"

She glanced over her shoulder, but said nothing. He thought maybe he'd already lost this round. Then just when he started to close the door, he heard her say in a soft, whispery voice, "Mariah."

Before he could respond, she rushed down the stairs. With her name echoing inside his head, he closed the door. Mariah. The name suited her. Somehow he sensed that beneath that cool, controlled exterior, a wild, untamed woman existed. But was she a woman who could be persuaded, with the proper inducement, to change alliances?

Figuring the odds, Jake decided that if Mariah was as much woman as he suspected she was, she could definitely be his best hope of getting out of this predicament, not only alive, but free from the Coalition.

Two

Mariah had been handpicked for this job because of her background in the Intelligence Division and her doctorate in psychology. If she succeeded at this crucial assignment, a promotion wasn't out of the question. Being young—only thirty—and female, she had to work twice as hard to prove herself. But competition and hard work were in her blood, inherited from her parents and instilled in her by her three older brothers. Her reputation as a hard-nosed professional who gave as good as she got only scratched the surface of the person she really was, the woman inside her who had spent a lifetime trying to prove she was the equal of her brothers and every man in her line of work. Her physical appearance alone intimidated some men. After all, at five-ten she was as tall as half the male population, and her physical prowess and expertise in the martial arts as well as practically every type of weaponry made her the equal of and often superior to a great many men.

As she removed Jake Ingram's clothes from the washer and tossed them into the dryer, she asked herself why she was rehashing old information. Her life had been on a steady, straightforward track since she'd graduated from college and chosen her profession. Having witnessed her parents' strong, happy marriage, she had secretly hoped that by now she would have found a man with whom to share her life. It wasn't as if she didn't date, although she'd been dating less and less these past few years as she'd concentrated on advancing her career.

Be honest with yourself, Mariah's inner voice demanded. You've given up dating because every suitable man you meet is either too awed or too intimidated by you to be a true partner. Most men like less aggressive women. Women who can't whip their butts. Women who can't outsmart them and outshoot them on a firing range. But Mariah refused to lower her standards. If she couldn't find a man with whom she could be an equal partner, she'd stay single and unattached for the rest of her life.

Mariah scolded herself. Now was not the time to be thinking about her sex life—or lack thereof. She was on an assignment. Lives were at stake. The security of U.S. citizens was at risk. So why had she allowed her unwanted attraction to Jake Ingram to send her libido into overdrive and her thoughts wandering into forbidden territory? Yes, the guy was drop-dead gorgeous and masculine to the nth degree. So what? He was a key player in her assignment, not a potential lover.

She groaned silently. Don't even go there! But her mind had already painted a rather vivid picture inside her head—of Jake Ingram naked, aroused and dragging her down onto one of the twin beds upstairs. Great, just what she didn't need, a mental image of her being ravished by the man the Coalition expected her to break down mentally by slow, precise degrees until he cooperated fully and could be reprogrammed to do their bidding.

"Damn," Mariah cursed quietly under her breath.

"Got a problem, Doc?"

Gasping, Mariah turned and glared at Lester, who stood in the hallway outside the laundry room. "Don't ever sneak up on me like that again."

"Sorry, didn't mean to startle you. Burgess sent me back here to see if you need us for anything—" he rolled his eyes toward the ceiling "—up there."

"No, thank you." Mariah punched the timer on the dryer. "Mr. Ingram is taking a shower and shaving. I plan to carry his supper upstairs to him and then have a preliminary talk with him tonight."

"Aren't you going to start screwing around inside his head tonight?" When Lester grinned, a bit too lasciviously to suit Mariah, he revealed a set of crooked yellow teeth.

Mariah breathed deeply. This man was an idiot. "Mr. Ingram will respond more positively to my hypnosis therapy if he's well fed and well rested. I'll begin my brainwashing of the patient in the morning."

"Brainwashing, huh? I thought Burgess said you were supposed to reprogram him. But I guess it's all brainwashing, isn't it?" With one hand braced against the door frame, Les leaned into the laundry room, his gaze traveling from Mariah's face to her breasts. "I'm sure glad you aren't going to be messing around inside my head. But if there's any other part of me you'd like to mess with, I'd be more than obliging."

Mariah pursed her lips tightly, just barely controlling her rage. She'd love to tell this moron exactly what she'd enjoy doing to him, but since he was working for the Coalition, it was in her best interest not to antagonize either him or his partner. But stroking this man's ego wasn't part of the deal.

"Look, Lester, we're both here to do a job," she told him. "And if you don't stop harassing me, I'll report you to our superiors. Do I make myself clear?"

"Yeah, honey, I get what you're saying. We're both working and you don't go in for any hanky-panky on the job."

She could correct him, but she didn't. Instead she gave him a cold, calculated glare. He grinned, nodded and then walked away. She sighed. Thank goodness. Maybe he'd leave her alone. If not, she'd have to deal with him less diplomatically.

When she entered the kitchen, she went straight to the refrigerator and quickly removed the ingredients for two sandwiches. If she shared dinner with Jake Ingram, she could accomplish two objectives. One, not having to come back downstairs for a while and deal with Les and Burgess. Two, sharing something as social as a meal with her captive might make him less hostile tomorrow. Working quickly, she prepared two ham and Swiss sandwiches, added a pile of potato chips and dill pickles to each plate. She poured two large glasses of cola, then as an afterthought, she reached up into the cabinet next to the microwave and pulled out a bag of pecan shortbread cookies. She removed four cookies and laid them on the counter. After placing all the items on a serving tray, she added a couple of paper napkins.

All her life Mariah had been blessed with a healthy appetite and a great metabolism. Even now, out of her twenties, she never worried about her weight. But part of maintaining a toned, healthy body came from regular exercise. And she prided herself on staying physically and mentally fit.

As she headed out of the kitchen, she saw Les hovering in the hallway. Doing her best to ignore him, she started up the stairs.

"Don't you want me to carry that up for you?" Les asked. "Looks mighty heavy for—"

"I can manage just fine. Thank you." Picking up her pace as fast as she could with the extra burden of a heavy tray, she didn't look back at the leering man. And even without eyes in the back of her head, she knew he was ogling her.

"Get the hell back in here and leave the doc alone," Burgess yelled. "If she needs us, she'll let us know."

Mariah said a silent thanks to Burgess. When she

reached the upstairs hall, she noticed that both the bathroom and the bedroom doors stood wide open. She glanced into the bedroom. Wearing the white terry-cloth robe she'd given him, Jake lay sprawled out atop the spread on the twin bed to the left. He'd crossed his long, hairy legs at the ankles, and his head rested in the cushion of his cupped palms created by his entwined fingers. His eyes were closed, but she doubted he was asleep. His thick black hair glistened with moisture. Odd, Mariah thought, the man looked as if he didn't have a care in the world, as if he were at some swank hotel and was resting peacefully after his shower.

She cleared her throat. He opened his eyes and looked right at her.

"I brought our supper up here," she told him as she entered the room.

He rose from the bed and came toward her. "Let me take that tray."

"No, thank you," she replied. "I don't need any help."

He shrugged.

She placed the tray on the desk. "Come on over and sit down. You should eat and then try to get some sleep." She pulled out the wooden desk chair, then walked over to the corner and dragged the over-stuffed armchair to the end of the desk.

Jake sat where she'd instructed him to sit, glanced at the meal she'd prepared and picked up a glass of cola. He downed half the glass before he set it back down and grabbed the sandwich. By the time Mariah sat, he'd devoured a third of the ham and Swiss.

"Slow down," she cautioned. "You're eating on an empty stomach and if you eat too fast, you might make yourself sick."

Jake grabbed a napkin, wiped his mouth and grinned. "Are you always so bossy?"

"Yes," she said without hesitation. "It's part of my charm."

"But only part." His gaze raked over her in a sensual, beckoning way.

Her nipples tightened. Thank goodness she was wearing a good bra and a bulky sweater. "Yes, only part. I'm also patient and persistent. I usually accomplish whatever I set out to do."

"Usually, but not always?" Jake munched on the potato chips.

Mariah picked up her sandwich, but before taking a bite, she said, "I win more often than I lose."

"Hmm. What's your average?"

Mariah chewed and swallowed, then grasped her glass of cola. "My average? I'd say at least eighty percent or more."

Jake looked skeptical, then let out a long, low whistle. "Are you a sore loser?"

"Depends."

"On how gracious your opponent is in victory?"

"On whether or not my opponent plays by the rules."

"But the same principle doesn't apply for you,

does it?'' Jake said. ''Working for the Coalition is definitely not playing by the rules. They're a rogue organization. A threat to our government.''

''According to you.''

''Are you telling me that a smart lady such as yourself actually believes in the Coalition's ultimate goals?''

''I believe in doing my job,'' Mariah told him, being as truthful as she dared.

''And just what is your job? To brainwash me into working for the Coalition?'' When she didn't respond, he went on. ''Don't waste your time. All the mind games you have in your repertoire won't work on me.''

''I expect you to resist,'' she told him. ''I've done my homework on you, Jake. I know everything there is to know about you.''

Jake centered his gaze on her face, studying her closely. ''You only think you know everything about me. You know facts. That's all. Height, weight, shoe size. Where I went to college. What I do for a living. Who my biological parents are. But, lady, you don't know me. If you did, you wouldn't even try getting inside my head. I won't let you in.''

''Not willingly. But there are methods.''

''I'll fight you, every inch of the way.''

Yes, of course he would. She knew that about him, too, as she knew all those other facts about his life. He was a strong, stubborn man, who, like she, always played to win. And from what she'd read about him, his average was higher than hers. About ninety-five percent. He bested her by ten to fifteen percent. But this time, she had to win. What Jake didn't understand—what she couldn't explain to him, at least not yet—was that both their lives depended on her pulling this deal off to perfection. Or at least as near to perfection as humanly possible.

"Why don't we just enjoy our meal together," Mariah suggested. "There's no need to discuss unpleasant matters tonight. I want you to rest, relax and try not to worry." Damn, Mariah, what an asinine thing to say to the man. He's been beaten, kidnapped, is being held captive and expects you to try to brainwash him.

Jake chuckled. "Just what are you willing to do to help me relax tonight?"

Damn man! He was as bad as Lester with his sexual innuendoes. Yeah, but there was one major difference—no way in hell would she ever fantasize about Lester making love to her.

"I'd be happy to give you a sleeping pill or—"

Jake laughed out loud.

Mariah hadn't blushed in at least ten years, but heaven help her, she felt the heat of embarrassment warming her cheeks. "You men are all alike. Take your mind out of the gutter, Mr. Ingram."

"Your mind must have been in the gutter, too," he told her. "Otherwise, you wouldn't have known why I was laughing."

Mariah stood, pushed the chair back into the corner, then walked toward the door. "I'll check on your clothes. They should be dry soon. Why don't you finish your supper while I'm gone."

"Say good-night to Lester and Burgess for me, will you? Tell them to sleep tight and not let the bedbugs bite."

Mariah huffed. "Did anyone ever tell you that you have a very warped sense of humor?"

Before he could reply, she escaped. Her plan to stay upstairs as long as possible this evening went up in smoke. But she was running scared—away from Jake Ingram. Fending off Lester's unwanted advances was a piece of cake compared to indulging in sexual repartée with her captive.

Jake ate hungrily, finishing his sandwich and chips in a couple of minutes. As he toyed with one of the shortbread cookies, he thought about escaping. Not tonight. But soon. And if what he suspected was true—that Mariah was attracted to him—he'd just have to find a way to use her to implement his escape. Who knew if she might help him or even go with him? But persuading her could take days. Or longer. What he didn't have was time. No matter how well he managed to resist the doctor's mental probing, sooner or later, the Coalition would expect results. If Dr. Brooks couldn't manage to brainwash him, they would try other methods.

Before he could use Mariah, he had to get to know her, learn what her weaknesses were. On the surface, she didn't seem the type to join a group like the Coalition. But then he didn't really know her political views, her religious preferences, her heart's desire or her soul's passion. What he needed was a crash course in Dr. Mariah Brooks. And he'd often found that sex was the quickest way to become acquainted.

Sex. Jake harrumphed. He'd been celibate ever since Tara had ended their engagement. It wasn't that she'd broken his heart when she'd called off their wedding. Hell, he had postponed it several times himself, coming up with one good excuse after another. The bottom line was that Tara and he hadn't been right for each other. He'd never really looked beyond that successful, beautiful, cultured facade she presented to the world and seen the self-centered, self-serving bitch beneath the glossy exterior. Maybe he'd known all along that when the chips were down, Tara wasn't the kind who'd stand by her man.

Finding out that he'd been born as a result of genetic engineering had unnerved her. Oh, she'd hidden her revulsion well enough, but he'd known. He'd felt her rejection in his gut. She didn't want to be married to a freak, no matter if he did possess certain superhuman qualities.

It wasn't that he'd intended to swear off women and give up sex; he'd simply needed a little time to let the wounds heal. He'd thought he was in love with Tara. Hell, maybe on some superficial level, he had been. After all, the lady had looked damn good on his arm. She'd been the type of woman everyone thought a man in his position should have. And perhaps the rich, willowy blonde had been exactly what the old Jake had deserved. But he was no longer the same man he'd been a year ago. He knew the truth about his heritage, had met his biological brothers and sisters, and was fighting the demons who had destroyed his birth parents and had manipulated their lives. Jake hoped he was a better person for the experiences he'd endured. Maybe the new, improved Jake deserved someone vastly different from Tara Linden. Someday. In the distant future. When he'd straightened out his life. When he and his siblings were safe. When the Coalition had been annihilated.

But before he could move forward into that idyllic future, he had to take care of his present problems. And the first order of business was escape.

Bide your time, he told himself. Let Dr. Brooks think you're playing into her hands, then manipulate her for your own purposes. No matter how attracted you are to her, never forget that she's the enemy!

With Jake's warm, clean clothes in her arms, Mariah said good-night again to Lester and Burgess. This time, Lester seemed rather subdued; no doubt the result of Burgess's previous warnings. At least that was one irritation she wouldn't have to deal with again this evening. But upstairs, waiting for her, was a situation she wasn't sure how to handle. Her intuition and training warned her that Jake Ingram was playing her, that he'd picked up on her attraction to him and was trying to figure out a way to use it to his advantage. But unless she had misjudged his feelings, Jake wasn't immune to her either. There was most definitely some chemistry there—like a live wire sizzling between them.

Why now? she asked herself. And why with this man? Wrong time. Wrong place. But the big question remained—under different circumstances, would Jake Ingram be the wrong man? What does it matter? she asked herself. Deal with the problem. Don't let it get out of hand. She was a trained professional, not some horny, sex-starved woman out to get laid.

By the time she reached the door to the bedroom she would share with Jake tonight, she had herself convinced she could handle her overactive libido and do the job she'd been sent here to do. Even after getting another good look at Jake, who still sat in the chair at the desk, her resolve remained firm. After all, it wasn't as if he was the first good-looking man who'd ever come on to her.

She placed his folded garments on the foot of his bed. "You can get dressed while I take my shower."

"Aren't you going to handcuff me to the bed?" he asked flippantly.

"If you try to make a break for it while I'm in the shower, Burgess and Lester will probably shoot you. So I don't recommend an escape. At least not tonight." She tried for the same humor he'd used.

"All right. Not tonight." He scooted back the

chair and stood, then walked across the room. "But maybe tomorrow night."

She shook her head. "Not tomorrow night either. Why don't you wait until I tell you when."

He gave her a puzzled look, then grinned, assuming she was joking. For just a moment she thought he was coming toward her, but he paused, glanced down at his clothes on the bed and said, "Are we going to bed soon?"

"What?"

"I was just thinking there would be no point in putting on my clothes if we're going to bed soon."

"Uh, yes, I—I see." Oh, great, Mariah, get tongued-tied at the mention of you two going to bed. He didn't mean go to bed together. Or did he? "You can just put on your underwear and get in bed. It's early, but I have a busy day planned for us tomorrow."

"I don't sleep in my underwear," he told her.

"What do you— No. Absolutely not. If you're accustomed to sleeping in the raw, forget it. Put on your shorts and T-shirt."

"Is that an order, Madam Warden?"

"Yes, that's an order."

When Jake sat on the bed, Mariah hurried to the closet, removed her pajamas, robe and slippers, then scurried across the hall to the bathroom. Once inside, she closed and locked the door, then stood there with her back braced against the door until her accelerated breathing calmed.

She took her time showering and washing her hair, hoping that when she returned to the bedroom, Jake would be asleep. After her shower, when she was drying her hair, she picked her watch up off the edge of the sink. Nine-fifteen. Over an hour had passed. She groaned. Who was she kidding? Jake wouldn't be asleep. He'd be lying there in the bed next to hers, wide awake and waiting for their next verbal sparring match.

When Mariah opened the bathroom door, she hesitated, then reminded herself of who she was and the importance of her assignment. No way could she allow personal issues to cloud her judgment. She marched into the bedroom, closed the door behind her and, deliberately not looking at Jake's bed, walked straight to hers. She removed her velour robe, tossed it on the foot of her bed, turned down the covers and placed her gun under her pillow.

"Even in those ugly flannel pajamas, you can't hide that great body," Jake said.

"I'm not trying to hide anything," she told him. "I'm trying to stay warm."

"If staying warm is a problem, I have a solution."

Her mistake was looking at him. He sat up in bed, his pillow against the headboard, his broad, bare chest totally exposed.

"Where's your T-shirt?" she asked. "You'll need it to stay warm." She used a hand gesture to request he not make any suggestions on how they could stay warm.

"I don't sleep in a T-shirt." He scratched his hairy chest. "The damn thing presses against my hair and makes my chest itch."

"Well, you're in the Arizona mountains in the dead of winter. I suggest you put on your T-shirt and scratch. It's better than freezing half to death."

As hard as she tried, she couldn't immediately remove her gaze from those broad shoulders, that muscular chest, those big, fined-toned arms or that washboard belly. Fully clothed, Jake Ingram was a handsome devil. Undressed, he was devastating.

Jake tossed back the covers. Mariah held her breath, uncertain whether he was wearing his shorts. Thankfully, he was. She sighed quietly. He jerked the white T-shirt from atop his jeans and plaid flannel shirt lying in a neat pile on the floor, then pulled it over his head. It was then that Mariah noticed the dark bruises along his side. Oh, God, he'd been severely beaten. When he glanced at her, his gaze narrowed and a hint of a smile played at the corners of his mouth.

"You were wondering if I had on my shorts, weren't you?"

"They beat you," she said, her gaze fixed on his bruised side.

"Yes, ma'am, they did."

"Do you think you have any broken ribs?"

He shook his head. "I'm not in agonizing pain, so I figure my ribs are still intact."

"There was no need for them to do that to you."

"I'm afraid there was. You see, I resisted."

"Of course you did." Putting a damper on her desire, she rushed to him to check his bruises for herself, to make sure he wasn't badly injured. Bad move! She wasn't supposed to care what had happened to him. You're not playing your part very well, she told herself. Act unconcerned, dammit!

Mariah retrieved the handcuffs she had removed from Jake earlier and walked over to his bed. She hated having to cuff him to the headboard, but if he tried to escape, Lester or Burgess would stop him, maybe even kill him. She couldn't allow anything to happen to Jake. He was too valuable. Part of her job was to keep him safe.

"Sorry to have to do this, but…"

He held up both arms. She hesitated, wondering how touching him would affect her. Just do it, she told herself. She grabbed his left arm, cuffed his wrist and then attached the other cuff to the bedpost. Frozen to the spot, the feel of his warm wrist still tingling through her palm, she stared at him, and from the way he was looking at her, she suspected that innocent touch had rattled him as much as it had her. If not, then he was doing a damn good job of faking it.

"If you need to go to the bathroom during the night, or need anything else, just let me know," she said.

"I'll keep the offer in mind."

Once again he'd used her own words against her,

changing their original intent into something sexual. Let it go, she told herself. Don't respond.

Mariah slid into bed, pulled the covers up to her waist, then reached out to turn off the bedside lamp. "I'm going to sleep," she told him. "I suggest you do the same."

Several minutes later, when her eyes adjusted to the darkness, Mariah could see a sliver of light coming from beneath the closed door. She lay there, wide awake and wishing she was anywhere else on earth. Anywhere except confined inside a mountain cabin with a man she had to think of as her enemy. A man who, come morning, she would be forced to deceive, playing with his mind the way a cat plays with a mouse before going in for the kill.

Three

Much to his surprise, Jake actually slept several hours before waking with a cramp in his arm. When he first awoke, he tugged on his wrist and couldn't figure out why it was bound, but then reality hit him like a splash of ice-cold water. Everything came back in an instant flash. His beating, capture and transport to this isolated mountain cabin. Using his free hand, he massaged his aching arm; then as he flipped over, he glanced at the person lying in the bed next to him. Dr. Mariah Brooks. The woman fascinated him, but he didn't have the luxury of fully exploring that fascination. What he needed from her—and needed as soon a possible—was her help in escaping. Accomplishing that goal would take finesse on his part. If he pushed too hard, too fast, she might balk. But then again, he really couldn't wait.

He wondered how deeply involved she was with the Coalition, how many years she'd been working for them. Was she doing it for the money or was she committed to their cause? If it was money, he could offer her twice what they were paying her. If it was a true commitment on her part, then he might be screwed. Unless he could charm her into helping him, regardless of her loyalty to an unjust cause. Women had been known to betray their families, their countries, their own valued principles, all for love. Could he seduce Mariah into thinking she was in love with him? He didn't have much time. He needed to put a plan into motion immediately.

"Dr. Brooks?" Jake called her name softly, but when she didn't respond, he said it a bit louder the second time. He could barely make out her dark form moving beneath the covers, but when she turned over, he felt certain she was looking his way.

"Is something wrong?" she asked, her voice sleep-husky.

"I've got a cramp in my arm," he admitted honestly. "Would you mind removing the handcuff for a few minutes?"

"All right." As soon as she rolled out of bed, she flipped on the bedside lamp, lighting the room with a forty-watt creamy white glow.

He watched her as she got to her feet—long slender feet, with red toenails. Red toenails! Now wasn't that interesting? Dr. Brooks's fingernails were short and sported clear polish. Neat, professional, boring. But her toenails were fire-engine red. Bright, sexy, ultrafeminine. And exciting.

She retrieved the key for the handcuffs, then approached his bed. He looked up at her and smiled. "Did anyone ever tell you that you're awfully pretty when you first wake up?"

Narrowing her gaze to slits, she glowered at him

as she reached down, unlocked the handcuffs, removed one cuff from the bedpost and then pulled the other cuff from his wrist. He dropped his arm and sighed dramatically while he rubbed his arm from wrist to elbow.

"I don't know what sort of game you think you're playing," she said, "but I advise you to forget it."

As she turned to walk away, he reached out, grabbed her arm and dragged her down until she toppled over on top of him. He wasn't quite sure what to expect, didn't know if she'd slap him, just jump up to get away from him or verbally reprimand him again. She surprised him by sliding off him and onto her side, then she stared deeply into his eyes. Those sky-blue eyes of hers appeared twice as bright, twice as sparkling, against the golden glow of her dark complexion. In that one instant of complete stillness, Jake slid his arm around her. She didn't move, didn't respond, and he realized she was holding her breath.

He caressed her neck with his fingertips. "Do you play chess, Mariah?"

She shook her head, tossing her thick black hair ever so slightly from side to side. "I jog, I play tennis, I work out at the gym. As far as games go, I haven't played any since I was a kid. Checkers and jacks were my favorites."

He continued caressing her, allowing his fingers to linger over her earlobe a few minutes before forking them through her hair. "In chess, each player's goal is to attack the enemy's king in such a way that the king can't escape. It's a game of wits. You must learn to not only evaluate your own moves, but you must anticipate your opponent's next move."

"Does chess have anything to do with the game you're trying to play with me?" A shiver rippled through her when he cupped the back of her head and brought his mouth within a hairbreadth of hers.

"What do you think?"

"I think you should release me and go back to sleep. I plan to start our first session fairly early in the morning."

"Why don't we start now?" Before she had a chance to respond, he lowered his mouth and kissed her. Gently. Sweetly. Being careful not to seem too aggressive. For a split second she responded, giving herself over to the moment, but then she ended things. Abruptly. Withdrawing quickly, she stared at him, a startled expression widening her eyes.

"No." She uttered that one word before she pulled out of his arms and shot up off the bed. After turning from him, her back ramrod straight, she stood in place for several seconds before she faced him again. Without saying anything else, she grabbed his arm, manacled his wrist and yanked the cuffed hand high enough to secure the other cuff to the bedpost.

Jake looked up at her, but she wouldn't meet his gaze. He'd had her there for a few seconds. She'd been his completely. Perhaps he'd been too gentle. Next time—and there would be a next time—he'd take her hard and fast, without giving her a chance to think.

"Should I apologize?" he asked.

Instead of responding, she turned and walked away, straight back to her bed. She dropped the key into her boot, which rested on the floor beside her bed. He watched her while she crawled beneath the covers and then switched off the lamp.

"Mariah?"

Silence.

"I don't like it any more than you do, you know," he told her. "How do you think I feel being attracted to a woman who plans to try to reactivate Oliver Grimble's programming embedded in my brain? Believe me, lady, you're the last woman on earth I want getting me hot and bothered." Say something, damn it, Jake thought. Had he really blown it with Mariah? Had the kiss been too much too soon? "We can't help it. Neither of us. I want you. You want me. It's that simple. We'll have to find a way to deal with it."

"Go to sleep, Jake," she said finally, her voice low and calm. "You need your rest."

"Avoiding talking about it isn't going to change anything. It's not going to make us want each other any less."

"Shut up, will you?"

Smiling, Jake burrowed his head into the fluffy pillow. He had her rattled. He considered his options and decided that keeping quiet was the wisest course of action right now. Mariah was interested, but she was no pushover. She would fight him every inch of the way. And if he knew women—and he did—she'd be cool and aloof come morning. He expected her to give him the cold shoulder and probably take a bit of perverse delight in trying to break down his defenses. His gut instincts told him that Dr. Mariah Brooks was accustomed to being the one in charge. Maybe he should let her believe she could control him, then when she least expected it, make his move.

Mariah brought Jake downstairs for breakfast with Burgess and Lester, an action designed to deactivate Jake's out-of-control libido. Of course, she wasn't sure whether the guy really was turned on by her or if his seduction routine was simply part of some master plan he'd concocted. Either way, she had to make sure he didn't kiss her again. In the wee hours of the morning, she'd known before he kissed her that he was going to—and she'd let him. She'd had enough warning so she could have stopped him if she'd really wanted to. But that was the problem—she had wanted that kiss. Her own sexuality and curiosity had gotten the best of her, at least for a couple of seconds. Thank goodness she'd been able to use her common sense in the nick of time. Another couple of seconds and she would have been lost. As it was, just that brief kiss had been enough to curl her toes. Heaven help her, she was "in lust" with Jake Ingram. Talk about a major professional mistake!

"Will you need us to go upstairs and stay with you this morning while you work on Ingram?" Burgess, who stood beside the kitchen counter, downed the last drops of his second cup of coffee, then put the empty cup in the sink.

"Not unless Mr. Ingram refuses to cooperate," Mariah replied.

"You're not going to do that, are you, buddy boy?" Standing at the back of Jake's chair, Lester ruffled Jake's hair.

Jake snarled, then glanced over his shoulder and gave Les a warning glare.

"I plan to give Mr. Ingram an injection," Mariah said. "Burgess, perhaps you should accompany us upstairs to make sure he doesn't give me any trouble. Once the medicine takes effect, I should be able to handle things myself."

"What are you going to give him, some type of truth serum?" Les asked, his lopsided, yellow-toothed grin difficult to stomach so early in the morning.

"What type of medication I use on Mr. Ingram is none of your concern. You're here strictly to follow my orders and I'm ordering you to mind your own business."

"Humph!" Les glowered at Mariah, but he didn't respond verbally.

She looked at Burgess. "I'm going to set things up in the bedroom and I'd like for you to bring Mr.

Ingram upstairs in a few minutes. I'll let you know when.''

"Yes, ma'am." With a nod of his head, Burgess motioned for Les to leave the room, which he did immediately, if somewhat reluctantly. "I'm sorry Les is giving you a hard time, Dr. Brooks. He thinks he's a damn ladies' man."

"I appreciate your keeping him in line," Mariah said. "But I do plan to report his behavior to our superiors."

"I understand."

"These corn flakes could use a little something," Jake said.

Both Mariah and Burgess snapped around and glared at him.

"Maybe a banana or some blueberries or—"

"You're lucky you're getting breakfast," Mariah told him. "Some forms of therapy use deprivation as a tool. No sleep. No food. No privacy. I'm being very lenient with you, Jake. I expect you to appreciate my kindness."

Jake stared at her, puzzlement in his eyes, then suddenly he smiled. Damn the man. It was as if he could see right through her, as if he understood what motivated her, why she was treating him so coldly this morning. He might suspect that she was protecting herself from her unwanted attraction to him, and he'd be right. But he didn't know the half of it, had no idea why she couldn't allow either Burgess or Lester to think she was going easy on him. And with the Coalitions' two goons nearby all the time, she couldn't risk explaining herself fully to Jake because she didn't know how he'd react. For that they needed totally privacy, which meant she had to find a way to get Jake's bodyguards out of the house for a few hours.

"I'd like to speak to you privately," Mariah said to Burgess. "Would you mind stepping out into the hall for a few minutes."

"Les, get your ass back in here and keep an eye on Ingram," Burgess bellowed.

Les came running like an obedient dog. Burgess motioned to Mariah to walk into the hall, which she did. He followed right behind her.

"Yeah, what's up, Doc?" Realizing what he'd said, Burgess chuckled.

Mariah laughed, faking amusement. "If everything goes the way I think it will today, Mr. Ingram will be exhausted and I'll be putting him to bed early tonight." Mariah looked directly at Burgess, keeping her tone friendly yet commanding. "Unless something unexpected comes up, I don't see why you and Les shouldn't get out of the house for a few hours, maybe drive into town to the local bar. According to the weather forecast, they aren't predicting any snow for a couple of days, so this evening might be a good time to take a break, in case we get snowed in here later."

"We just might do that. Les is already antsy.

Maybe if he finds him a woman tonight, he'll stop pestering you.''

"Soothing the raging beast in Lester sounds like a good idea.''

"Are you sure you'll be all right alone with Ingram?''

"I'm positive.'' She faked a wide smile. "I plan to give him a sedative this evening and it will knock him out for the night.''

"Okay. You go on and get things ready. Then just let me know when you want me to bring Ingram up to the bedroom.''

Mariah nodded. "Thanks.''

She hurried upstairs, all the while thinking about the act she was about to perform. She knew enough about hypnosis to realize that it worked on about twenty-five percent of the general population, those individuals known as a "suggestible person.'' The other seventy-five percent could be made susceptible to mental manipulation by the use of drugs. She didn't intend to waste her time with the standard hypnosis tricks. With a stubborn, self-confident man like Jake, she would have to use drugs if she hoped to achieve the desired effect. But first, she had to set the stage for Jake, and to make it look totally real for Burgess and Lester.

After placing the medical bag on her neatly made twin bed, she opened the satchel and prepared two syringes. The first medication would calm Jake, relax him into a state of drowsiness. The second was a top-secret drug—secret to Burgess and Lester.

After securing the blinds over the windows, Mariah turned on the two fluorescent lights that she'd arranged on either side of the desk. The lights weren't too dim nor were they too harsh and would be conducive to helping Jake relax. After that, she set up the portable CD player and popped in a tape she had prepared that repeated a lulling instrumental tune, the beat mimicking the rhythm of the human heart at approximately fifty-five beats per minute.

With the room set for her patient, she walked to the head of the stairs and called, "Burgess, please turn the thermostat down by ten degrees. I want the upstairs to be slightly cooler than normal. If you two get chilly, just put on your coats."

"Yes, ma'am," Burgess replied. "Are you ready for Ingram now?"

"Give me a couple of minutes, then bring him up."

Everything was as ready as it could be—everything but her. She'd never done something like this and wasn't sure just how good an actress she was. This is a part of your job, she reminded herself. You'll do what you have to do.

Mariah rushed into the bathroom and closed the door. After using the facility, she washed her hands and took a good, hard look in the mirror. Did she look as scared as she felt? No, she didn't. Thank goodness. It wasn't as if she hadn't been involved in numerous difficult and dangerous assignments—she had. But this one was different and more difficult than she'd anticipated. Because of Jake Ingram. She certainly hadn't expected to be instantly attracted to the guy. More attracted to him than she'd ever been to any man, especially on such short acquaintance.

Just remember that what you're doing will, in the long run, save Jake's life.

When she emerged from the bathroom, she met Burgess and Jake in the hall. For some reason Jake didn't look like a condemned man, and he should. Damn but he was arrogant self-assured.

"Bring him into the bedroom and sit him in the chair at the desk," Mariah said.

Burgess nodded, then prodded Jake, who obediently went into the bedroom and sat down in the chair. He sat with his back straight, his chin tilted, appearing totally unafraid and just a bit too confident to suit Mariah. He was up to something, had some devious plan in the back of his brilliant mind. She hoped he didn't do something stupid, something that would necessitate Burgess and Lester playing rough. A major part of her job was to keep Jake alive, and unharmed if at all possible.

"Jake, I'm going to give you an injection," Mariah said. "Please, roll up your sleeve."

He glared at her, then looked pointedly at the hypodermic syringe she picked up out of the medical bag. "Mind telling me exactly what's in that thing?"

"It's simply a mild solution that will help you relax," she explained.

"And that's it? Just a little something to put me in the mood?"

"Yes, something like that." Mariah picked up on the double entendre, but knew Burgess hadn't. Neither Coalition bodyguard had any idea that something highly sexual and extremely personal was going on between Jake and her. And she intended to keep it that way. Business first, then if they both came out of this alive, there might be time for Jake and her to explore their mutual desires.

Jake rolled up his sleeve and held out his arm. So compliant. So agreeable. Didn't the man understand that he was as susceptible to the effects of medication as any ordinary mortal? He might be the product of genetic engineering and possess superior intelligence, but he was still a human being. Was he so sure he had bewitched her, that she would do him no harm? Was his ego really that huge? Or did he suspect the truth? Had he figured out who she really was?

With a steady hand, far calmer than her rioting nerves, she gave him the first injection, then separated the needle from the syringe and placed it in a safety container.

"How long before it takes effect?" Burgess asked.

"Almost immediately," Mariah replied.

Within minutes Jake's eyelids drooped and his breathing slowed. When she placed her hand on his shoulder, he glanced up at her and grinned. And every feminine instinct within her wanted to reassure him that she wasn't going to harm him, that he was safe with her.

"I'm feeling a bit woozy, Doc," Jake told her.

"Good. That's how you're supposed to feel." Mariah reached inside the medical bag and removed the second hypodermic.

Jake's eyes widened for a moment and he pressed against the back of the chair, as if he were trying to move away from her. "I thought you said only one injection."

"The first one was to relax you." She walked over, gently rubbed his arm and pointed the needle. "This one will make you more cooperative."

"It won't work," he said. "I'm not going to let you get inside my head."

"We'll see." She injected him with the secret drug, then glanced at Burgess, who seemed totally enthralled by the whole procedure. "Thank you, but I should be able to take it from here. You may go back downstairs. If I need you, I'll let you know."

"Yes, ma'am."

As soon as she heard Burgess's heavy footsteps trudging down the stairs, Mariah closed the bedroom door. She was way out of her league on this type of procedure, so all she could do was pretend she knew what she was doing. In other words, fake it.

"You've got everything set up just right, don't you?" Jake's words weren't slurred, but he spoke slowly, as if talking took great effort. "The right lighting…the monotonous, heartbeat rhythm…the cool temperature. What next, Doc—a voice roll?''

"How very astute of you, Jake," Mariah said, deliberately pacing her words so that they rolled off her tongue at approximately sixty beats per minute. "You seem to know a little something about hypnosis techniques."

"Want to tell me what was in the second hypodermic? So far, I haven't felt any effects."

"You won't," she told him. "Not yet."

"I don't know of any drug that—"

She clamped her hand on his shoulder. "It's an old remedy. Tried and true. It works on most patients."

"Is that right?"

"Just relax, let your mind drift and think about something pleasant."

"I can do that. Let me see." When Jake tried to lift his arm, he found the task rather difficult, but managed to lay his hand over his heart. "I'll think about escaping. That's a pleasant thought." He reached up and laid his hand on hers where she gripped his shoulder. "Or I could think about making love to you. An equally delectable thought."

"Whichever you'd like. Anything pleasant will do." How she kept her voice steady, she didn't know. Just hearing him say the words "making love to you" put erotic images in her mind. "Are you relaxed?"

"Mmm."

"Are you thinking of something pleasant?"

His hand inched backward until he was able to caress her hip. "Very pleasant."

After removing her hand from his shoulder, she moved backward, just enough so she was out of his reach. "Now, Jake, I want you to count backward for me, beginning with one hundred."

He chuckled softly. But he didn't start counting.

"Jake, did you hear me?"

"Tell me what was in the second syringe and I might count for you."

"You don't want me to bring Burgess back upstairs, do you?"

"You wouldn't do that."

"And just what makes you think I wouldn't?"

"Because you don't want him or anyone else to hurt me. Do you, Mariah."

"Please, count backward for me."

"What was in the second syringe?"

Mariah breathed deeply, then took a calculated risk and decided to tell Jake the truth.

She went over to him, leaned down and whispered in his ear, "I injected you with a secret superdrug, one that has cured many ills for numerous patients over the years. The second injection was a placebo."

Four

Jake woke with a start. He didn't even remember having dozed off. The last thing he recalled was Mariah doing her level best to hypnotize him. Burgess had checked on them once by himself, then a second time with Lester. Each time they'd had an audience, Mariah had voiced her aggravation with Jake and her commitment to keep at him until she'd broken him down. When they were alone, she'd been less aggressive, although persistent. And he always sensed that she was putting on a performance, even when they were alone.

"He's resisting," she'd told Burgess and Lester, her voice stern. "I've never dealt with a more stubborn, determined patient. It's going to take time to wear down his resistance, but sooner or later, I'll get what I want from him."

As Jake glanced around the room, he realized he was lying in bed, atop the bedspread. How had he gotten here? He'd been sitting upright in a chair during the hypnosis sessions. Had Mariah managed to put him to bed by herself, or had the big, muscle-bound Burgess assisted her? Undoubtedly the good doctor had been lying to him when she'd told him the second syringe had contained a placebo. Either that or the first injection had been a time-released type of drug that had taken a couple of hours to render him unconscious. Either way, he knew one thing for certain—even under the influence of a drug, he hadn't yielded to pressure, hadn't succumbed to any type of mind control. However, there was one thing he wasn't certain about—curious about, definitely, but completely uncertain. And that was Dr. Mariah Brooks herself. His sixth sense—call it intuition, gut instincts or whatever—told him she was not the enemy, but his common sense told him she was. Friend or foe? She had treated him well, but that could be simply because she was attracted to him. Or was playing him for a fool? He suspected that although she wasn't familiar with the game of chess, she had the type of personality conducive to mind games. On the other hand, if she wasn't serious about reprogramming him for the Coalition, she certainly put on a convincing act whenever Burgess and Lester were around.

Jake surveyed the room and found it not only quiet and semidark, but empty. He heard a radio playing downstairs, which meant he wasn't alone in the house. Where was Mariah? Making a report to the Coalition on her failure to manipulate Jake Ingram? When he rose into a sitting position, he was pleasantly surprised to find that he wasn't groggy in the least. And he wasn't bound, neither his hands nor his feet. When his stomach growled, he remembered that he hadn't eaten lunch today, and glancing out the window, he realized the sun would soon be setting. Had he slept through the noon meal and most of the afternoon? Apparently he had.

Too bad there wasn't an easy escape route from the second floor. Now would be the perfect time to make a run for it. Jake got out of bed. When his feet hit the floor, he realized he still wore his boots. What were the odds that he could sneak down the stairs, make it into the garage and steal a vehicle before getting caught? Jake chuckled to himself. The odds weren't in his favor.

Moving quietly, he made his way across the room, eased open the door and visually explored the hall. Empty. He entered the hallway, then crept over to the stairs. Stopping at the top, he listened. Voices. Burgess and Les. He took several tentative steps downward, then paused. Mariah was speaking.

"Please, don't worry about me. I'll be fine here alone with Mr. Ingram," Mariah said. "The third injection I gave him put him out like a light. He'll sleep all night."

"Come on, Burgess, let's go," Les said. "If the weather gets nasty tomorrow or the next day, tonight could turn out to be our only chance to go into town and kick up our heels."

"Maybe I should call headquarters to make sure it's all right." Burgess's uncertainty reflected plainly in his voice.

"There's no need to do that," Mariah told him.

"I'm in charge and you're to follow my instructions without question. Is that understood?"

"Yes, ma'am," Les and Burgess replied simultaneously.

"Then stop worrying and just go. I have your cell phone numbers if I need you. And if you get any flak from our superiors, I'll take full blame."

What was going on? Jake wondered. Why was Mariah so eager to get rid of Burgess and Lester? A self-satisfied grin curved his lips. Did the lady have a little hanky-panky in mind? There was nothing he'd like better. And for more than one reason. Did he want to have sex with Mariah? You bet he did. But more importantly, their being totally alone for several hours would give him the opportunity to use some gentle persuasion on her. And if gentleness didn't work, he'd simply overpower her and make his escape alone. Either way, he intended to be a free man before midnight.

Backtracking, Jake made his way up the stairs and into the bedroom he shared with Mariah. No need to do anything hasty and foolish. All he had to do was wait. Wait for Mariah to come to him.

Mariah stood at the kitchen door and waved good-bye to Burgess and Lester, a phony smile plastered on her face. The minute they pulled out of the garage, she closed the door and rushed through the house and into the living room. Standing at the row of floor-to-ceiling windows at the front of the cabin, she watched until she was sure they were out of sight. She didn't dare move too quickly. All it would take was one mistake to put her mission in jeopardy. But tonight might well be her one and only chance.

She wondered if Jake was still asleep. Surely he was awake by now. The first injection she'd given him had relaxed him and muddled his thought processes slightly. The second was only a placebo, something she'd convinced Burgess and Lester would assist her in her assignment to reprogram their prisoner. Just as she'd known he would do, Jake had resisted all her attempts to hypnotize him. And she suspected that even a real doctor would have no better luck. Jake was totally in control of his mind, even his subconscious, so much so that he wasn't susceptible to reprogramming. And once the Coalition realized he would be of no use to them, they would have only two choices—either kill him or find another way to control him.

Mariah figured she had several hours—two at the least, four at the most—to convince Jake of her true identity and persuade him to trust her. Without any credentials, Jake would have to take her at her word. But why should he?

You're going to help him escape, aren't you? she asked herself. If that doesn't convince him, nothing will. But what if he thinks you're trying to trick him?

She'd taken a couple of steps up the stairs when the telephone rang. Her muscles tensed. She doubted it was Burgess and Lester, so that left only one other possibility. When she lifted the receiver and said hello, the voice at the other end of the line gave her a name and a code word that immediately identified him as a Coalition agent.

"How did the first session with your patient go?"

"Not well," she replied. "He's fighting me every inch of the way. It will take time to break him down."

"We don't have time to waste."

"I can't accomplish the reprogramming quickly. It could take weeks to—"

"I suggest you use another tactic. We now have a secret weapon that should make your patient totally cooperative."

Fear clutched Mariah's chest tightly. What secret weapon? "That's good to hear. Exactly what sort of—"

Once again interrupting her, the man said, "Tell your patient that we are entertaining a special guest here at headquarters. The brother he sacrificed himself to save is once again back in the fold, so to speak. Tell him that his brother's life depends on his cooperation."

"My God, you have—" The Coalition had captured Gideon Faulkner! How would Jake react when he learned that his great sacrifice had been for naught? He'd been willing to risk not only his freedom, but his own life to save his brother. Now the Coalition had Gideon and planned to use him as a bargaining tool to manipulate Jake. "Yes, I understand. You most certainly have the only secret weapon that would make my patient cooperate.''

''Then use that weapon, Dr. Brooks. I will contact you tomorrow evening to see how your second session went. I expect it will go much better than today's session since you will be able to give him a reason to cooperate fully. All most people need is the right incentive.''

''Yes, sir. I look forward to your next call.''

''And I will be eager to hear your progress report.''

When she hung up the receiver, she stared at her hand and marveled at how steady it was. Inside she was shaking like a leaf. She had to get Jake out of here tonight. Tomorrow would be too late. But if she told him about Gideon, what would his reaction be? She was ninety-nine percent sure she already knew. From what she'd learned about Jake through the extensive files she'd researched and from their brief yet intimate acquaintance, she figured Jake would insist on trying to save his brother. But she couldn't allow him to do that.

Gideon was quite valuable to the Coalition, but Jake was even more so. Jake Ingram was the quintessential superhuman. Although his genetic makeup varied only slightly from his siblings, the experimental genetic engineering Dr. Henry Bloomfield had performed had created children who each possessed their own unique talents. In Jake's case that genetic tinkering had resulted in a multitude of physical and

mental abilities, not the least of which was his
genius-level mathematical mind and his perfect body.
The guy was drop-dead gorgeous, physically superb
and ruled a multi-billion dollar firm as an international financier. Of all the siblings, Jake was the one
the Coalition wanted most. And it was her job to
make sure they would never be able to use him. She
had to keep him safe, even if it meant sacrificing his
brother.

Where the hell was Mariah? Jake had heard a vehicle leaving about fifteen minutes ago, and from
what he could make out, it looked like Burgess's
SUV. Then only moments after the Saturn had disappeared down the road, the phone had rung. What
was going on? Something was happening, something
Jake didn't think he'd like. Were they planning on
moving him? Were Burgess and Lester being replaced? Was that the reason Mariah had sent them
into town? He had thought seduction might have
been Mariah's motive, but now he wasn't so sure.
Of all his special abilities, reading women wasn't one
of them. He'd been dead wrong about Tara. What
made him think he had Mariah pegged right? He had
planned to use the physical attraction she felt for him
to his advantage. But what if she had plans of her
own—plans to use him?

Do you dare risk taking the chance? he asked himself. Why not strike first and ask questions later? After all, he was a man, which meant he was physically

stronger. All he needed was a slight edge, something to counterbalance the fact that she had a gun.

Suddenly he heard footsteps on the stairs. Mariah? He inched his way to the open bedroom door and peered around the corner. His heart pounded in his ears. The element of surprise could give him the advantage he needed. She wouldn't know for sure he was awake, would have no reason to have her weapon drawn.

He slid to the side, waiting quietly against the wall. She came closer and closer, her footsteps tapping softly on the wooden floor. A crazy thought zipped through his mind. He didn't want to hurt her, only subdue her. Dammit, man, why do you care? She is the enemy!

Or is she?

"Jake?"

He tensed the moment she called his name.

"Jake, are you awake?"

He could feel her drawing close, almost at the door now.

"We need to talk," Mariah said.

The second she stepped over the threshold and entered the semidark bedroom, Jake grabbed her, his arms wrapping around her like a vise.

"What the—"

"I'm leaving here—tonight," Jake growled the statement in her ear.

"Let go of me," she told him. "Do it now."

"No way, honey."

"Trust me, Jake. I can help you. Just release me."

"I don't trust you any farther than I can throw you."

She wriggled. He tightened his hold. She winced.

Without any warning, Mariah went into defense mode, and before Jake knew what was happening, she performed a couple of expert maneuvers that kicked him on his ass. Reacting instantly, Jake came back at her with equal skill. Mariah gave as good as she got and within a few minutes both were perspiring and glaring at each other.

"Give up, Dr. Brooks," Jake said. "You can't win. Not against me."

"Damn you, Jake. We don't have to do this. If you'd just listen—"

"Listen to lies? No, thanks. I've heard enough lies to last a lifetime. Hell, my whole life has been a lie."

He knew that she wasn't going to give up, not until he had subdued her completely. He had no choice but to finish this fight. They battled for several more minutes. Mariah's skill impressed him. But in the end, he managed to toss her onto the bed and pin her down. The more she struggled against him, the more aroused he became. His sex was hard and throbbing, and getting more so with every stroke of her body against his.

"Stop fighting me," he told her. "You'll only hurt yourself. And I don't want you to get hurt."

She looked up at him, her expression softening as

her chest rose and fell with her slightly labored breath. "Jake…"

Ah, hell. How could he resist her? She'd fought him like a pro, which she probably was. But she had accepted defeat, hadn't she? And from the hungry look in her big blue eyes, he could tell she wanted him as desperately as he wanted her. When all was said and done, she could tell herself that she'd put up a good fight, but Jake knew she was his now—his for the taking. And he most certainly intended to take her.

Common sense flew out the window as Jake lowered his mouth to hers. She sucked in a deep breath. His tongue glided in a circular motion, surrounding her lips. She sighed. Her hips lifted, pushing her mound firmly against his erection. When his lips brushed across hers, she closed her eyes and opened her mouth. Jake took her actions as an invitation and delved his tongue inside her moist, welcoming warmth. He wanted to taste her, touch her, every inch of that long, lean body. He longed to discover for himself how full and firm her breasts were, how hot and wet her femininity was, how wild she'd be when he buried himself inside her.

She not only accepted his kiss, but returned it, sending her tongue into play. When he loosened his hold on her to slip one hand between them in order to fondle her breast, she eased her arms free, then lifted one hand to caress the back of his head. He deepened the kiss, devouring her, longing to strip her naked and take her quickly. He was hurting so bad he didn't know how much longer he could hold out. He hadn't been this horny since he'd been a teenager with raging hormones.

When he nuzzled the top of her shirt where it lay open just below her throat, she whimpered. And when he began undoing the buttons, she squirmed against him, sliding her legs up and down his. Just as he managed to jerk her shirt from her slacks and loosen the final button, Mariah lifted her leg and kneed him in the groin. Jake yelped. He saw stars as the pain radiated through his body. Mariah shoved him aside and jumped to her feet. Jake writhed in agony for a couple of minutes, then rolled over on the bed and glared up at her.

"I should have known," he said. "Your compliance was just a ploy to get away from me, wasn't it?"

Mariah inhaled strongly, then released the breath. Perspiration dampened her face and throat. A pink flush colored her cheeks. Her blouse gaped open, revealing a simple white cotton bra filled to capacity with a pair of large, round breasts. Jake forced himself to move his gaze from the swell of those luscious breasts to her face. He felt like kicking himself. Or better yet, pinning a big sign on his back that read Sucker!

"If you plan on keeping me under control, you'd better use your gun." Jake eyed the hip holster she wore. Why the hell hadn't he removed the damn thing when he'd had the chance? Because he'd been too damn worked up about the prospect of getting laid.

"Jake, please listen to me. I'm not your enemy. You've got to trust me. We don't have much time. I have no idea how long Burgess and Lester will stay in town."

Jake sat on the edge of the bed as the pain subsided. "You want me to trust you? You've got to be kidding."

Mariah came forward, but paused several feet from the bed. "I want to sit down beside you and talk to you calmly. Promise me you won't do anything stupid."

Jake chuckled sarcastically. "I've already done something stupid. I let you outsmart me. I had you right where I wanted you—" He ended his sentence abruptly when he realized that he had indeed had her where he'd wanted her. Flat on her back, lying beneath him, ready for sex.

"Look, Jake, you're not the only one confused by the way we react to each other. Believe it or not, having the hots for you complicates my job immensely. You have no idea."

"Not exactly Coalition procedure to hop into the sack with your kidnap victim, huh?"

"I don't work for the Coalition," Mariah told him.

"Is that so?" He eyed her skeptically.

"I really need you to believe me. We have only a brief window of time when we can leave here and

get a head start before Burgess and Lester return.''
Mariah hurried to the closet, removed their coats
from hangers and tossed his coat to him. When he
made no move to put it on, she huffed. ''Come on.
Let's go.''

Jake took his time putting on his coat and standing
up, all the while amused by Mariah's nervousness.
When he finally walked over to her, he asked, ''So,
you don't work for the Coalition, huh?''

''That's right.''

''Then, Dr. Brooks, would you mind telling me
why they sent you here to try to reprogram me?''

''First of all, I'm not Dr. Brooks. I'm not a doctor
of any kind, certainly not a psychiatrist. And sec-
ondly my name is not Mariah Brooks. It's Mariah
Daley.''

He stared at her quizzically. ''Let me get this
straight. You're not a doctor, not a psychiatrist, your
name isn't Brooks and you aren't a member of the
Coalition?''

''That's right.''

''Okay. Then who are you and what the hell are
you doing here?''

''I told you, I'm Mariah Daley. Special Agent Mariah Daley.''

''Are you saying you're an FBI agent?''

She nodded.

''I don't understand—''

''The Coalition is a threat to national security. The
FBI has been investigating the organization for quite

some time and after the World Bank Heist, the bureau sent in several agents to infiltrate the group. I was actually put in place as a psychiatrist to help your brother Gideon, if and when the occasion arose. But once you were kidnapped, I volunteered for the job of reprogramming you."

"You expect me to simply take your word that you're an FBI agent."

"My mission was to protect you and get you out of here as soon as possible. That's what I'm trying to do…if you'll cooperate."

"If you're really a federal agent, then you must know that there's no way I'm running away to safety before I retrieve a very valuable item from Coalition headquarters."

"Gideon's disk will be retrieved, but not by you," she said. "You're far too valuable for us to allow you to take such a dangerous risk. We will handle things from the inside once we locate the Coalition's new headquarters here in Arizona."

Jake reached out and cupped Mariah's chin. "The Coalition has moved its headquarters?"

She nodded. "The bureau will discover the location soon, I'm sure. Then we'll do what has to be done from the inside."

"When we leave here we're going straight to their new headquarters to get Gideon's disk and to access the disk that will cut off the Coalition accounts. You'll need me—need my expertise."

"No way. I'm taking you to a safe place, where

the Coalition can't find you. You'll have to leave the rest to us. Besides, I told you that we don't know the exact location—''

"You wouldn't lie to me, would you? You can find out what your superiors know. And I'll bet they have a good idea where the new Coalition head-quarters might be." Jake eased his hand from her chin, down her throat and then across to her shoulder. Gripping gently, he squeezed her upper arm. "I'm afraid you're mistaken, Special Agent Daley, if you think you're the one in charge. We'll do this my way or we won't do it."

"What do you mean, we won't do it?"

"I mean I'll stay right here until Burgess and Les-ter return, unless you agree to my terms."

Mariah blew out an exasperated breath. "Are you crazy? Tonight is probably our only chance of es-caping and you're wasting time arguing over who goes in to retrieve Gideon's disk?"

"That's right, honey. Either I do it or—"

"Why does it have to be you?"

"Because apparently none of your undercover agents have been able to retrieve it, have you? I know exactly what I'm looking for and I'm not afraid to risk everything to get what I want."

"We'll get that disk, when the time is right. But until then—"

Taking a defiant stance, Jake crossed his arms over his chest. "Make this easy on both of us, Special Agent Daley, and agree to what I want. If you do, we can leave right now. And if you don't want to assist me, then once we're away from this place, you can drop me at the nearest bus depot—after you tell me where the Coalition has moved their headquarters. You go your way and I'll go mine.''

''What makes you think that's an option?''

''Apparently you're afraid of going after the disk. Afraid to blow your cover. So be it.'' Jake shrugged. ''I'll go in alone while you report back to your boss.''

''If you think for one minute that I'd let you go in alone and risk your life, then you don't know me, mister. I'd never desert you that way.''

Jake grinned. When he reached out to caress her cheek, she shivered. ''Is that your way of saying you're the kind of woman who stands by her man?''

''Don't make this personal.''

''Too late. Anything that happens between us is personal and there's not a damn thing either of us can do about it.''

''We can't risk your falling into enemy hands again.'' Mariah looked at him pleadingly. ''Try to see things from my point of view.''

''We agree on one thing—we shouldn't waste any more time arguing.'' He grabbed her wrist. ''Come on. Let's head out of here. We can argue about our destination on the way.''

She hesitated, then nodded. Not for one minute did he think he'd won the war, only this one battle. Later, once they were miles away from this place, he'd find a way to persuade her to come around to his way of thinking. If not, he'd have to overpower her again and head off on his own.

When they reached the kitchen, Mariah paused before unlocking the back door that led into the garage. "About halfway down this mountain, there's a back road we can take so we can bypass Flagstaff and hit I-40 about forty-five miles from here."

Jake held out his hand. "I'll drive."

She narrowed her gaze and frowned.

"Come on, hand over the keys." He wiggled his fingers.

She reached in her pocket, pulled out the keys and held them out to him, but when he reached for them, she closed them up in her palm.

"What?" he asked.

"You drive, but I'll navigate. I can get us off this mountain and to the interstate with little chance of running into Burgess and Lester."

"Agreed."

Lifting her clutched fingers, she opened her palm to him. He grabbed the keys, placed his hand in the center of her back and urged her into motion. Just as they reached the garage and Jake hit the button on the keypad to unlock Mariah's Chevy TrailBlazer, they heard the sound of a vehicle and saw the flash of headlights through the side windows in the garage.

"What the hell? That can't be Burgess and Lester," Jake said.

Five

Jake recognized the voices immediately. Lester's grumbling, midwestern drawl and Burgess's gruff, I'm-in-charge growl. Damn! What the hell had sent these two back to the cabin in such a hurry? They hadn't been gone much more than thirty minutes.

"Give me your gun," Jake whispered to Mariah. "We'll get the jump on them when they come in the back door."

"No, we won't. They both have weapons and they're both killers. I can't take any unnecessary risks with your life."

"Dammit, woman, you're too cautious to be a federal agent. They may have weapons and be trained killers, but they're idiots. I say we—"

Before Jake knew what hit him, Mariah gave him a couple of well-aimed chops to his midsection and his jaw, sending him to his knees. When he glanced up, she was holding her pistol on him, a threatening look in her eyes. Just as he opened his mouth to ask her what the hell she was doing, the kitchen door opened. Burgess stopped dead in his tracks. Lester skidded directly into Burgess's broad back.

Burgess looked down at Jake, then surveyed Mariah from head to toe and noticed they were both wearing coats. "What the hell's going on here?"

"Mr. Ingram tried to escape," Mariah said convincingly. "I'd stepped outside for a few minutes to look for a tape I thought I had in my car and caught him trying to slip out just as I came back in." Mariah pointed her 9 mm right in Jake's face. "You should know better than to try to escape. Did you think that because I'm a woman, I couldn't stop you?"

"Damn bitch," Jake grumbled, falling into the pretense mode Mariah was using, and wished she'd take her gun out of his face.

Easing the gun to her side, Mariah turned to Burgess. "Help him get up, then take him upstairs." Burgess jerked Jake roughly to his feet. "And be sure you handcuff him to the bed. He can sleep in his clothes for all I care. I'm through being nice to him. Obviously he doesn't respond to good treatment."

"Hey, Doc, if you want me to work him over, just say the word," Lester offered.

"Thanks, but I don't believe that will be necessary. At least not tonight."

Burgess grabbed Jake by the nape of his neck. "I thought that shot you gave him would keep him sleeping all through the night. What happened?"

"I don't know, unless his genetically altered system is more resistant to the drug than the average person. If I use it again, I'll increase the dosage."

Mariah lied quite nicely, Jake thought.

"He don't look much like a superhero right now."
Lester got right up in Jake's face and grinned. "How
does it feel, Mr. Big Shot Genius, having a woman
best you?" When Lester chuckled manically and
Jake smelled his sour breath, he wanted to coldcock
the son of a bitch.

"Get him upstairs," Mariah ordered.

When Burgess yanked Jake into motion, he didn't
resist. As bad as he hated to admit it, Mariah had
probably been right to have responded quickly and
subdued him before he'd acted on pure male instinct
and attacked the two men when they entered the
kitchen. It was possible he might have been able to
shoot Burgess, wounding or killing him, but before
either he or Mariah could have gotten to Lester, the
guy would have pulled his gun and opened fire.

"Oh, by the way, why are you two back so soon?"
Mariah asked. "You didn't even have time to make
it into town."

Lester chuckled again, with more humor and less
menace this time. "Our big tough guy here—" he
pointed at Burgess "—got a bellyache and we had
to stop and let him go by the side of the road. He's
got the backdoor trots."

"Shut your trap!" Burgess gave his partner an
I'm-going-to-kill-you glare.

Lester kept laughing, the grating sound reverber-
ating throughout the cabin. Mariah returned her
Smith & Wesson to its holster, then headed to the
refrigerator. She hadn't eaten since lunch and Jake

hadn't had a bite since breakfast. She removed a couple of apples from the crisper, then brought out a hunk of cheddar cheese, sliced off several thick slabs and laid them on a paper towel. All the while Lester watched her, his leery grin unnerving her even more than her watchdogs' unexpected return.

"Get away from me!" She snapped around and glowered at the aggravating man. "Go to your room, watch TV, go take a flying leap off the nearest mountain peak."

"I like a feisty woman. I don't mind a good fight before the sex."

"Out!" Mariah yelled. "Get out of my sight. Now!"

Count to ten. Recite the Lord's Prayer. See how many U.S. presidents you can name, Mariah told herself. Do anything to stop yourself from killing Lester.

"Hell, you must be on the rag or something," he grumbled as he walked out of the kitchen.

After taking several calming breaths, she stashed the apples and wrapped cheese in her coat pocket and headed up the stairs. When she reached the hallway, she met Burgess coming out of her bedroom.

"I let him take off his coat before I handcuffed him to the bed," Burgess said. "If that's all you need me for right now, I—"

"Go, go." When Burgess rushed past her toward the stairs, she called out, "There's some Imodium in the kitchen cabinet over the sink, along with several other items in the first-aid kit."

"Yeah, thanks."

After entering the bedroom, Mariah closed the door quietly behind her, then held up a finger to Jake to indicate silence. Jake, one wrist chained to the bedpost, nodded his understanding. She locked the door, then removed the food items from her pocket and placed them on the desk.

"I couldn't fix you a meal since I've stated that I'm preparing to use some not-so-nice tactics on you," she said softly. "But I did bring up apples and cheese for myself and there's enough for two."

"I guess I should apologize for suggesting we gun it out with those two." Jake grunted. "I'm usually not so foolhardy. Or at least I didn't used to be. Something in me seems to have changed drastically since I discovered the truth about my past. I've always been known for my logical thinking, for being cool under fire, but lately I've been jumping into action and disregarding the danger to myself."

"You want to protect your siblings. Gideon in particular right now. And you want to help bring down the Coalition. That's perfectly understandable." Mariah took off her coat and tossed it on the bed, then walked over to Jake, the key in her hand, and unlocked the handcuff attached to the bedpost.

"What if one of our bodyguards comes up here to check on us?" Jake asked as she moved to unlock the manacle on his wrist. "Maybe I should keep the cuff on so I can stake myself out again if we hear them coming."

Mariah paused. "Burgess will be in and out of the bathroom for hours. And I believe Lester is wondering whether or not I'd actually shoot him. But maybe you're right." She left the handcuff on his wrist.

Jake grinned. "He just doesn't know when to give up, does he?"

"You're right about him. The man's an idiot."

Jake got up, clutched Mariah's shoulder and squeezed. "Let's eat while we work on Plan B."

"What's Plan B?" she asked.

Jake sauntered over to the desk, pulled out a chair and sat, then picked up an apple and bit into it. After chewing and swallowing, he replied, "The next escape plan. Surely you have a backup scenario figured out."

"I'm thinking knockout drops in their morning coffee."

Jake smiled.

"If possible I'll do it in the morning," Mariah said. "If not tomorrow, then the next day. As soon as I can work out something to keep both men out of the kitchen long enough for me to doctor the coffee and think of a good excuse for not drinking any myself."

"Maybe I can do something to distract them. I don't mind getting roughed up a bit, as long as it's for a good cause."

"We'll play it by ear in the morning. Now eat, then we need to get some rest. I'll set the alarm so we can get up early. Maybe I'll whip up some pancakes or something and be all female and fluttering in the morning. And you can act up when I give you a cue. Get wild enough so that it'll take both Burgess and Lester to drag you out of the kitchen.''

Jake munched on the apple. Mariah sat on the edge of the desk and unfolded the paper towel protecting the cheese. When she held out her hand, offering him a slice of cheese, he eased up off the chair just enough to bring his lips in alignment with hers. She held her breath, waiting for his kiss.

Without breaking intimate eye contact with her, he took a piece of cheese, then whispered against her mouth, "Thanks.''

Tension wound tightly inside Mariah. "You're welcome.'' Even to her own ears, her voice sounded sultry and breathy. God, why was it that when he got so close to her, she turned into a hundred percent female, without a hint of the tough, highly trained federal agent about her? He brought out all her feminine instincts, reverting her into a primitive woman who needed a man for survival. Snap out of it right this minute, her common sense warned.

He eased back down in the chair without kissing her. Hit by a combination of bemusement and frustration, Mariah laid the paper towel on the desk and picked up the second apple. What was Jake playing now? she wondered. Hard to get? If so, then she'd simply turn the tables on him. Two can play that game.

Jeez, Mariah Colleen Daley, what's the matter

with you? Even with Jake she couldn't shake the highly competitive side of her personality. She'd been born and bred on competition, a natural side effect of being not only the baby of four children, but the only girl in a family of three brothers. She'd had to fight, scratch, claw and play rough in order to survive. And as far back as she could remember, she'd thrived on keeping up with her brothers and doing her damnedest to outdo them. Her father, a Hillsboro, Ohio cop, had loved the fact that his daughter was a real scrapper. And although she and her mother, a Southern gal from Lexington, Kentucky, had always maintained a close relationship, Mariah had hero-worshiped her father. Heck, the whole town of Hillsboro had admired big Mike Daley.

Mariah eased off the desk and strolled across the room, then flopped down on her bed and bit into the apple. Now wasn't the time for playing games. And it certainly wasn't the time to compete—in any way, shape, form or fashion—with the man it was her sworn duty to protect. But try as she might, she found it difficult to see Jake Ingram as a helpless victim. Despite being kidnapped with his life now in constant danger, he didn't possess the demeanor of a victim. And even handcuffed and shackled, as he'd been when Burgess and Lester brought him to the cabin, he hadn't seemed helpless. It was that confident, self-assured attitude of his that made him seem invincible. Had that much self-confidence come naturally to him because he possessed a genius IQ?

"A penny for your thoughts," Jake said.

Mariah took another bite from the apple, chewed and swallowed. "You like to play games and I like to compete. I guess it's the same thing. There's always a winner and a loser. And neither of us likes to lose."

"And this great observation is leading up to...?"

"We shouldn't be playing games or competing. We need to cooperate. If we're going to get you safely away from the Coalition, we'll have to work together."

Jake nibbled on the cheese. "Hmmm."

"I'm the professional in this case. I believe you should follow my directions."

"Hmmm."

"Will you stop saying that!"

"You can plan the great escape tomorrow and I'll follow your directions to the letter," Jake told her. "But once we leave here, we're going to devise a plan to steal Gideon's disk from Coalition headquarters. And we'll do what can be done only from the inside—access the disk that will cut off the Coalition accounts."

"Leave that job to us. I've tried to explain how important your safety is to—"

"If you G-men—" Jake grinned "—could get to the disk, you'd already have it. So don't tell me to leave it to the professionals. I thought I'd made myself clear—nothing is more important to me than retrieving that disk.''

Is it more important than Gideon's life? she almost asked, but clenched her teeth before she blurted out the information that was sure to prompt Jake into acting foolishly. Put yourself in his place, she told herself. If the Coalition was holding Michael or Steven or Patrick, what would you do? A big part of your professionalism would get lost in your personal concern for your brother. You'd take foolish risks. You'd leap into action and consider yourself a one-woman army.

She had to keep the information about Gideon's capture from Jake—just until she had placed him under guard with a team of Federal agents to protect him. He'd probably hate her for lying to him by omission, but she'd do whatever she had to do to keep him safe. Mariah prided herself on being a top-notch agent. To date, she had an exemplary record, and her accomplishments had been rewarded with several promotions. But saving Jake Ingram had become more than just an assignment. It had become, much to her dismay, very personal.

''I understand how you feel,'' she told him. ''And I'm not going to waste my breath arguing with you. We need to concentrate on one goal at a time. And our first goal is to get away from here and out from under Burgess's and Lester's watchful eyes.''

''Agreed.'' Jake finished off his slice of cheese and chased it down with a last bite of apple. ''When

I get back to civilization, I want a steak as big as my head.''

''Would that be the actual size of your head or the figurative inflated ego size? The latter would mean a steak the size of Texas.'' Mariah took a huge bite out of her apple as she lifted her eyebrows and gave him a humorous glance.

Jake wiped his hands off on the wrinkled paper towel, then strode across the room, his gaze riveted to Mariah's face. She gulped. And when he was almost upon her, she tossed the apple core on the nightstand and started scooting backward, inching away from him. She wasn't afraid of him, not in the normal sense of the word. But the way she felt about him unnerved her. She really didn't like the fact that this guy could turn her inside out with just a bold look. It wasn't like her to go all gushy-gooey over a man.

Yeah, but Jake Ingram isn't just any man, she reminded herself. He's *the* man. Her maternal grandmother would have said, ''He's so Cary Grant.'' As far as Grandma Gloria was concerned, Cary Grant was the standard by which all other men on earth were judged. Mariah guessed there was a touch of Cary Grant in Jake, as well as a bit of Sean Connery's James Bond and maybe a hint of George Clooney's devil-may-care persona. And don't forget that the guy's a genius and about as physically perfect as a man can be, she reminded herself.

Keeping several inches separating their bodies,

Jake leaned over Mariah. "Since we have a very busy day planned for tomorrow, I'm ready for bed. How about you?"

Mariah swallowed, then nodded. "You in your bed and me in mine."

"Aw shucks, ma'am, we can't have no fun in two separate beds."

"We aren't going to have any fun. We're going to get a good night's sleep."

"How can I sleep in my condition?" He lifted himself up just enough to give her a full view of his aroused state.

She knew she had to stop their sexual bantering before it went any further. "Have you forgotten that Burgess and Lester are downstairs and both men carry very big guns? We're in a dangerous situation here and it's hardly the time for fooling around."

Jake swooped down over her, bracing his hands on either side of her head, the handcuffs dangling from his left wrist. He straddled her hips with his knees. "What better time to release some pent-up energy than when we're facing danger and maybe even death?"

He had spoken the words in a light, humorous tone, but when Mariah looked deep into his eyes, she saw how deadly serious he was.

"No, Jake, we can't."

"Yes, Mariah, we can."

"No. I'm a federal agent on an assignment. I can't—"

He cut off the rest of her sentence with a devouring kiss that took her breath away. The kiss was absolute perfection and had the desired effect. She melted like ice on asphalt in the summertime. Nothing could really be as wonderful as she thought this kiss was, could it? He continued the kiss, playing with her lips. Nipping. Licking. Oh, yes, this kiss was every bit as good as she thought it was. Maybe even better. When he eased his tongue inside, he slid his hand between them and undid the buttons on her shirt. She tossed back her head, exposing her throat and giving him a clear path from her lips, down her neck and to the front closure of her plain white bra. His quick, talented fingers undid the hook and shoved the cups away from her breasts. The dangling handcuff glided coolly over her hot skin. The moment he flicked his tongue across one nipple, she closed her eyes and sighed as her femininity clenched and unclenched.

Mariah wanted to touch his naked flesh. Tugging hard, she managed to free his shirt from his pants, enough to skim her palms up and over his rock-hard muscled chest. While exploring, she discovered a V-shaped thicket of curling hair that spread across his chest and down the center of his abdomen. She wanted to see him, but when he unsnapped her pants and slid his hand inside both her slacks and her panties, she bucked up, her body's needs quite obvious, as she forgot everything except her desire to have him bury himself deep inside her.

While Jake cupped her mound, she moved his shirt enough to kiss his neck and then his ear. He glided his fingers between her feminine lips and stroked her most sensitive spot. She writhed against his hand when he dipped two fingers inside her.

Nuzzling her neck, he whispered, "I love how hot and wet you are."

His fingers continued manipulating her intimately while his mouth moved from one breast to the other, giving each equal attention. A consummate lover, Jake knew how to bring a woman to the brink rather quickly. When she came, the explosion wild and fierce, Jake covered her mouth with his and captured her cry of satisfaction.

As she lay beneath him, panting and tingling while aftershocks rippled through her body, Mariah caressed his bulging sex through his pants. Jake eased off her and down on the bed beside her. When she turned over, she immediately reached for his belt buckle. No sooner had she released the buckle and unzipped his slacks than a loud knock pounded on the door.

"Hey, Doc, why have you got the door locked? You're not doing any unlawful experiments on our prisoner, are you?"

"Damn, it's Lester!" Mariah hissed the name through clenched teeth.

Six

"I happen to already be in my pajamas," Mariah responded. "Is there a reason why you've come upstairs to bother me?"

"Burgess is homesteading in the john, so he asked me to check on you before bedtime to make sure everything is okay with Ingram."

Jake shot off Mariah's bed, smoothed his shirt and plopped down on his bed, then handcuffed his wrist to the bedpost. Mariah undressed hurriedly, unconsciously giving Jake a quick striptease. He was already hard as a rock, and seeing her naked, no matter how briefly, made him break out in a cold sweat. If he didn't already want to rip Lester in two, the guy interrupting them at the worst possible moment—or was that the best possible moment?—was enough to bring out Jake's killer instincts.

After Mariah pulled her pajama bottoms up and jerked the top over her head, she glanced at Jake. The tension radiating between them was all but visible. Sexual energy charged the air. Mariah sucked in her breath, released it and headed toward the door, her bare feet padding softly on the wooden floor. She snapped the lock on the doorknob and cracked the door just enough to peer out at Lester. The little creep put his face up to hers and grinned. She jerked back in time to avoid their faces actually touching. If Lester had tried to kiss her, Jake figured she would have whipped his butt.

"Report back to Burgess that I have everything under control," Mariah said. "And tell him that I hope he feels better soon."

Lester grabbed the edge of the door. "You never did say why you locked the door."

"For privacy."

Lester grunted. "If Ingram got rowdy and you needed our help, we'd have to bust the door in, so how about keeping it unlocked?"

"Only if you swear to knock first and wait for me to open the door before you come barging in."

"That hurts my feelings, Doc. You're implying that I'm not a gentleman."

"Suffice to say that I'd never use your name and the world *gentleman* in the same sentence."

"You like talking all highfalutin, don't you? But I know an insult when I hear it." Lester shoved open the door, almost knocking Mariah down in the process. When she took a defensive stance, he paused just after crossing the threshold. "Maybe you prefer Ingram's company to mine since he's a genius and some sort of new and improved human being." Lester glared at Jake. "Hell, for all I know, maybe his John Thomas is twice the size of mine."

Jake wondered how long it would take before Mariah lost all patience with this jackass and put a couple of big knots on his thick skull. He could tell by the tense way she stood, her eyes narrowed to mere slits and just a hint of color in her cheeks, that she was ready to explode.

"Lester?" Mariah said his name in a sultry, feminine tone.

"Huh?" He snapped around and stared at her, melting into a puddle of white-trash desire.

She walked toward him. Slowly. A smile on her face. Then before Lester knew what had hit him, Mariah grabbed his arm, twisted it behind his back and added just the right amount of pressure.

"You're leaving this room." Forcing him into motion, she escorted him out into the hall. "You're going downstairs and you're not coming back up here tonight. Do you understand?"

Lester glowered at her. She increased the pressure on his arm. He struggled for half a second before the pain got the best of him and he yelped his surrender. "Okay. Okay. Don't break my friggin' arm."

"You be a good boy and leave me alone so I can sleep and I'll cook breakfast for you and Burgess in the morning." She gave Lester a none-too-gentle shove toward the stairs.

He didn't respond, didn't look back. His feet clomped loudly down the steps. Mariah returned to the bedroom and closed the door. But she didn't lock it.

"Lester could have waited awhile before barging

in," Jake said. "At least long enough for us to have finished what we'd started."

"I'm not sure he won't come back up here later. I've all but threatened to kill him, but he's like a dog with a favorite bone. He just won't leave me alone."

"Given the chance later on, if you don't beat the hell out of him, I'll be forced to do it myself."

Mariah grinned. "Do you need to go to the bathroom before I turn off the light and—"

"I don't need anything except more of you."

Mariah turned off the light. Moonlight stole into the room through the windows and cast golden black shadows across the floor. Jake slid down in bed until his head touched the pillow. He lay there atop the bedspread and tried not to think about the sight of Mariah naked or the feel of her in his arms or the taste of her on his lips.

Before his eyes adjusted to the semidarkness, he sensed her presence beside his bed.

"Mariah?"

"Don't talk," she told him as she reached out and unbuckled his belt.

"You'd better lock the door."

"No, I can't risk it."

"But it would be better for Lester to find the door locked again than to find us in a compromising situation."

"Just shut up, will you, and leave everything to me."

"Yes, ma'am!" Jake saluted her with his free hand.

Slowly, patiently, she unzipped his pants, eased her hand inside his briefs and freed his sex. When her hand circled his erection, he thought he'd die from the pleasure. But that pleasure was nothing compared to what happened next. Mariah crawled into his bed, positioned herself over the lower half of his body and ran her tongue over him from tip to base. Jake's hips bucked up and his sex jetted forward, begging for more. Much more.

After moistening him thoroughly and eliciting several deep moans from him, she took him into her mouth. Jake thought he would die. Pure sexual sensation radiated through his body. When she moved over him, up and down, sucking and licking, Jake knew he was a goner. All rational thought ceased to exist. In that moment he became nothing more than a mass of highly charged male energy. Virility to the max.

When she pumped him in and out of her mouth, he grabbed her head and encouraged her to take more. And she did.

Her mouth milked, her tongue stroked. And Jake came. It was all he could do not to roar with satisfaction. When his body calmed and the climatic spasms ceased, he grabbed the back of her neck and dragged her up over his body until she lay on top of him. Cupping the crown of her head, he kissed her passionately and tasted himself on her lips, in her mouth.

As he ended the kiss, he whispered her name. "Mariah."

"Shh. Don't say anything."

He kissed her again, but she was the one who ended it this time, then pulled away from him. He didn't try to stop her when she got up and went to her own bed. Silence filled the room.

"Thanks," he said.

She didn't respond. He figured she was as puzzled as he was by this hot, mad passion they felt for each other. He'd known a lot of women, but never anyone like Mariah. And never had he been as wild about a woman as he was about her. But the important question was would a fiery passion this intense soon burn itself out? Once they were out of danger, would their desire cool?

The next morning Mariah woke before six, checked on Jake and found him still asleep. As she headed for the bathroom, all she could think about was what had happened between them last night, when what she should have been thinking about was disabling Burgess and Lester so Jake and she could escape. She turned on the shower, stripped and stepped under the warm water. Her body responded when she touched herself with a soapy washcloth, all her senses recalling the feel of Jake's hands, mouth and tongue caressing her.

She was no novice to sex, although she'd been a late-bloomer, losing her virginity at twenty-three to an up-and-coming congressional aide. She'd dated Chip Larsen for nearly two years and they'd even talked about marriage somewhere down the road, but it hadn't worked out. She'd loved Chip, but… At the time, she hadn't been sure why their relationship had fizzled out, but in retrospect, she knew. They'd been young, both in exciting jobs, working with and socializing with interesting people. They had allowed their zest for life to dupe them into believing that fervor carried over into their love affair. But not once had Chip ever made her feel the overwhelming, uncontrollable lust she felt for Jake. Hell, no one had ever brought out the wild woman in her. She hadn't even known that part of her existed—not until she'd taken one look at Jake Ingram and every feminine instinct in her had gone into overdrive.

Okay, Mariah, so you've got it bad for this guy. Just don't go convincing yourself that it's anything more than sex. Especially not to him. Remember Jake Ingram is a superhuman, a nearly perfect specimen, physically and mentally. He could have his pick of women. Only recently he'd been engaged to Tara Linden, a successful corporate attorney and the daughter of a wealthy Texas tycoon. When Jake finally married, it would be to someone like his former fiancé—rich, gorgeous and socially prominent.

Mariah turned off the water, flung back the curtain, stepped out of the shower and grabbed a towel.

Wrapping her hair turban-fashion, she tried to vanquish thoughts of Jake from her mind. Common sense told her she'd made a major mistake in allowing her desire to override her professionalism. But her body—and yes, dammit, her heart—told her something else entirely.

Concentrate on business, she told herself. You've got to drug the coffee, make sure Burgess and Lester drink enough to knock them out, then get Jake away from the cabin and place him in the care of the bureau, where he would be safe from the Coalition. Unfortunately, she couldn't tell Jake about Gideon's capture until then, otherwise his hero mentality would demand he rush into harm's way and try to not only retrieve the invaluable disk, but save his brother.

After putting on her clothes, she went back to the bedroom and checked on Jake again, this time finding him awake and sitting up in bed.

"I'm going to head down to the kitchen and start breakfast." She went over to him and unlocked the handcuffs. "I'm hoping I can get the coffee made and doctored before Burgess and Lester get up."

"No good-morning kiss?"

Jake's beguiling grin was almost her undoing. Almost.

"No time for fun and games this morning. We've got more important things to do."

"I'll have to remember that you don't have a sense of humor early in the morning."

Despite her determination to remain unaffected by Jake's charm, Mariah had no control over her reaction. Having interpreted his comment to mean he expected they would be spending more early mornings together, her heart actually leaped for joy.

"I'm going to need your help," she told him, remaining cool toward him even though what she'd like to do was give him the good-morning kiss he'd requested.

"What do you want me to do?"

"Take a shower, get dressed and then come downstairs. If they're around, act subdued. Wait for my signal before you do anything. If I've already put the knockout drops in the coffee, I'll say something about not being hungry myself but hope they enjoy breakfast. If I haven't had a chance to doctor the coffee, then I'll say I've decided that you won't get any breakfast because I'm through being nice to you. That's when you can protest. Put up such a ruckus that it will take both Burgess and Lester to control you. I'll tell them to bring you back upstairs and shackle you to the bed again."

"I think I can handle that."

"I'm sure you can."

When she turned to leave, Jake grabbed her wrist. "About last night—"

She pulled free, but forced herself to meet his gaze head-on. "What about last night? No big deal. We fooled around a little bit. It's not as if it was the first time for either of us or as if it meant anything.

Right?'' Holding her breath, she waited for his response. A part of her wanted him to deny her assessment, wanted him to tell her that it had meant something to him.

Jake shrugged. ''Right. No big deal. Just sex.''

''Yes. Just sex.'' Before she got all female, all emotional, Mariah turned around and left the room. She managed not to run, although she needed to get away from Jake as fast as she could.

Just sex. Yeah, that was all it had been. For him.

Jake couldn't shake the feeling that he'd made a major mistake in passing off what had happened with Mariah as no big deal, just sex. But she'd been the one who'd said it hadn't meant anything. Yeah, Ingram, and you just automatically agreed, didn't you? No way were you going to risk denting your colossal male ego by admitting that there was something damn powerful happening between you two.

Jake tromped into the bathroom, stripped and got in the shower. While the warm water peppered over his back, he lathered his hair and tried to put all sexual thoughts of Mariah from his mind. Easier said than done. How did a guy forget about something so damn good, something that had, on a scale of one to ten, been an eleven? If oral sex had been that fantastic, what would it be like to bury himself deep inside her, to take her in the most basic, primitive way? Just the thought aroused him. Great. Just great. He'd awakened with a hard-on, but he'd managed to get it under control when Mariah had taken a shower. Now he had another erection. Bigger and better than the one before.

His life was in a mess. Kidnapped by the Coalition. His future on the line. The project his biological parents had created and for which each had died would possibly be reenacted to create another set of superkids—unless he and his siblings were able to stop the Coalition once and for all. He had to escape, make his way to secret Coalition headquarters and find Gideon's computer disk. So why in the middle of all this chaos had Mariah Daley come into his life? Wrong time. Wrong place. But the right woman. Romance should be the last thing on his mind. Not romance, he reminded himself. Just sex. Yeah, sure. Who was he kidding? He'd had ''just sex'' on quite a few occasions and he'd made love many times. He knew the difference. With Mariah, it was definitely making love.

But lovemaking usually required a level of intimacy that took longer than a couple of days acquaintance, at least in his experience. So why was it that after having met Mariah less than forty-eight hours ago, he found himself attached to her on an emotional level unlike anything he'd known in any previous relationship, short- or long-lived? Including his engagement to Tara.

Jake stepped out of the shower, dried off and dressed hurriedly. For now he had to forego psychoanalyzing his feelings for Mariah. First things first, he reminded himself. They had to escape, and that meant putting Burgess and Lester temporarily out of commission.

While he made his way downstairs, Jake recalled the cues Mariah had given him so he'd know whether to go berserk shortly after entering the kitchen or to keep a low profile. If Mariah could manage to drug the coffee, then there was a good chance her plan would work. Otherwise, they'd have to hatch a new escape strategy.

As he approached the kitchen door, he heard voices and knew Mariah was talking to the Coalition bodyguards. Before entering, he hesitated a couple of minutes and listened, but heard nothing but idle chit-chat. He kept his head bowed and his gaze downcast, following Mariah's instructions.

"Well, look here," Lester said. "Walking around free as a bird. What did you do to him last night, Doc, to make him so submissive?"

Burgess clamped his meaty hand down on Jake's shoulder. "What do you think she did? Isn't it obvious that she told him about his brother and he knows he's got to cooperate or else?"

Jake snapped his head up and glared at Burgess. What had he said? Something about Jake's brother? Did he mean Gideon? Jake looked toward Mariah, but she turned, faced the counter and began fiddling with the ingredients for their pancakes.

"What's he talking about?" Jake asked her.

"Just shut up," Mariah replied. "You don't ask

the questions. I do.'' She eased around slowly and shot him a warning glare. "And you might as well go back upstairs because I've decided that since you don't respond well to good treatment, I'll try a different tactic. From now on, no breakfast. As a matter of fact, no food at all—not until you cooperate fully.''

That was his cue to start a ruckus to distract these two goons so Mariah could doctor the coffee. But first he wanted her to explain what Burgess had meant when he'd said, "She told him about his brother."

"You heard the doc. Get going." Burgess gave Jake a none-too-gentle shove.

"If you aren't a good boy and jump whenever Doc tells you to, there's no telling what will happen to your brother," Lester said. "Ain't it just a kick in the pants to find out that you risked your life to keep Gideon Faulkner safe and now the Coalition's got both of you?"

For a couple of seconds all that registered in Jake's mind was Lester's cackling, maniacal laughter, but then realization dawned—the Coalition had captured Gideon. And Mariah knew about it. But she hadn't told him.

Jake stared at her and saw the truth plainly in her guilty expression. "You knew, damn you, you knew!"

"Shut up! I don't want to listen to your meaningless tirade," Mariah told him.

"He acts like he didn't know," Lester said, then turned to Mariah. "Didn't you tell him? We were told that you were instructed to inform Ingram that Gideon Faulkner had been captured and that if Ingram didn't follow orders, his brother would pay with his life."

"How could you have lied to me?" Jake demanded, thinking of nothing but the sense of betrayal he felt knowing Mariah hadn't been honest with him. He'd been a fool to think she was different—from Tara and all the other women he'd known. Mariah had her own personal agenda and what he wanted or needed was secondary to her assignment. "You damn bitch, you used me. You were going to—"

Before Jake realized her intention, Mariah crossed the room in a flash and crashed her fist into the side of his face, sending him reeling. For a couple of seconds, he saw stars. Literally. The lady certainly had a powerful punch.

Seven

After doing what she'd needed to do in order to silence Jake immediately, Mariah issued an order. "Take him back upstairs and cuff him to the bed. But gag him first. Once we've had breakfast, I'll start a new hypnosis session with him. And this time, I'm sure Mr. Ingram will cooperate fully."

Burgess grabbed Jake's arm, jerked him up from where he'd landed on his knees, and herded him toward the door.

After saying a silent prayer of thanks that Jake hadn't continued his tirade, Mariah turned her attention to Lester. "Go with them and—"

"No need," Burgess replied. "I can handle Ingram without any help."

Damn! Not only did she have to deal with Jake's reaction to finding out that Gideon had been captured by the Coalition and she hadn't shared that information with him, but now her plan to drug the coffee wasn't going to work, not with Lester remaining in the kitchen. So be it. She'd prepare the damn pancakes and undoctored coffee for Burgess and Lester, since she'd promised to fix breakfast for them this morning. But as soon as she'd wolfed down a few bites, she'd go upstairs and try her best to do some damage control. She had to find a way to make Jake understand why she hadn't been totally honest with him.

And just how do you propose to do that, Mariah? she asked herself. You've lied to him, albeit by omission. He's not going to trust you. There's a good chance that no matter what you tell him, he's not going to believe you. Dammit, she had to find some way to make him believe that she was on his side. One hundred percent. And there was only one way to do that—stand by him no matter what, and that included going with him to save Gideon!

How quickly this mission had changed for her, how quickly she'd gone from being an FBI agent doing her job to being a woman standing by her man. Idiot, she scolded herself, no matter what you do, Jake may never forgive you.

With robotic movements, she prepared breakfast, then served the meal when Burgess returned to the kitchen. Thankfully Lester had done nothing more than ogle her. Heaven help her, but if the man had come on to her again this morning, she might have reacted violently.

As she finished the third bite of syrup-drenched pancakes, Mariah glanced at the two Coalition flunkies who were thoroughly enjoying the fruits of her labors. She swallowed, then said, "I'm going to try to put Jake Ingram under a deep hypnotic trance and that procedure requires absolute concentration on my part and complete quiet. I don't want either of you bothering me while I'm working. Do you understand?'' She glared at Lester first, then at Burgess.

''We understand,'' Burgess said. ''But we'll be right here, ready to assist you if you give us the word.''

Mariah nodded, offered him a weak smile, then picked up her plate and headed for the kitchen garbage can. After dumping the contents of her plate, she placed the earthenware dish in the sink. Totally ignoring everything and everyone, her mind focused on how best to deal with Jake, she headed upstairs.

Please, God, don't let me screw this up. Too much depends on my making Jake understand.

When she reached the bedroom door, she paused outside. Her hand trembled ever so slightly as she grabbed the doorknob. What the hell was wrong with her? She wasn't the nervous, weak-in-the-knees type. Jake had most certainly done a number on her. And she didn't like it. Didn't like not being totally in control of her emotions. Didn't like letting her heart make her decisions instead of logic.

She eased open the door and gasped at the sight of Jake gagged, shackled to the bed and sporting a bruise on his right temple from where she'd hit him. But blood was also oozing from his swollen lip and there was a bright red spot on his jaw. Burgess must have taken it upon himself to rough Jake up a bit after he'd brought him upstairs. Damn the man!

Every feminine instinct within her urged her to run

to Jake, to comfort and care for him. So why was she so surprised by her reaction? After all, those womanly instincts had already chosen Jake Ingram as her mate. Her man. But she managed to control that nurturing urge as she entered the room. Jake looked at her, his eyes a turbulent, stormy blue and filled with pure rage. Mariah sighed. He wasn't going to make asking for his forgiveness easy.

Jake had never been this angry with a woman. Rage was a new emotion. He'd been bored, entertained, fascinated, hurt, disappointed, repulsed, delighted and even aggravated. But never angry enough to explode. It wasn't that no woman he'd been sexually involved with had never lied to him, but never a woman he'd trusted. And he had trusted Mariah. He had accepted her for who and what she claimed to be. And he'd mistakenly thought they had forged a bond—both physically and emotionally. Obviously he'd been wrong. He was nothing more to her than an assignment. Had her orders been to keep Jake Ingram not only safe, but pacified? Had she been told to do whatever necessary to make him cooperative? If so, then the FBI's methods weren't much better than the Coalition's.

Okay, so he wasn't thinking straight. He was allowing anger to overrule his usual logical thinking processes. He was reacting like a spurned lover. But learning that Mariah had lied to him about something as important as Gideon's life was as devastating as if he'd found her screwing around with another man. Both were betrayals. And the one thing Jake prized over everything else was loyalty. Complete loyalty. He expected it in his employees, in his family, in his friends and in his woman. He had been bitterly disappointed by Tara, whose loyalty and commitment hadn't endured the revelation about his unique birthright.

"Jake, we need to talk." Mariah paused in the middle of the room, as if waiting for his permission to come closer.

He glared at her. He wanted to shout, "Stay the hell away from me. You lied to me. You betrayed me. You're willing to let my brother die if that's what it takes to accomplish your mission!" But he said nothing. And couldn't if he tried, not with the gag in his mouth.

Mariah took several tentative steps toward him, then stopped by the side of his bed. It was a good thing his wrists were cuffed, otherwise he'd grab her and shake her until her teeth rattled. When she reached out and untied the handkerchief Burgess had used to gag him, a dozen different accusations came to mind. He'd thought he would bellow his condemnation of her the minute he could speak, but he didn't. Looking at her, seeing the stricken expression on her face, he realized two things. One: How he felt and what he thought truly mattered to her. Two: If she didn't mean so damn much to him, he wouldn't be this outraged over her betrayal.

"Jake, please, listen to me," Mariah said. "I'm sorry I didn't tell you about Gideon. I was wrong. I should have told you. But..." She crossed her arms over her chest and rubbed her hands up and down from elbows to shoulders in a nervous gesture. "My orders were to keep you safe, at any cost. I knew if I told you Gideon had been captured, you wouldn't escape with me, wouldn't go where you'd be safe— not until you found a way to free your brother."

"So you lied to me," he said. "You betrayed me. You would have taken me into custody and kept me under lock and key in order to protect me from the Coalition. It didn't matter to you that my brother's life is on the line." He narrowed his gaze and looked her right in the eye. "Do you have any idea how it makes me feel to know that my brother's life doesn't mean a damn thing to you?"

"That's not true." She held out her hands beseechingly, but made no attempt to touch him. "Gideon does matter to me, but not...not as much as you do. Your safety comes first with me."

"Don't you mean my safety comes first with the bureau?"

"Yes, keeping you out of Coalition hands is more important to the U.S. government than protecting Gideon. To them, you're the more valuable of the two. But wanting to keep you safe has become a personal issue with me. Can't you understand how important it is to me to protect you, to save you?"

"Why?" he asked, his gaze pensive, his voice hard.

"Why? Because I care about you."

"If you really cared, you wouldn't have lied to me."

"I've already apologized. I know I should have been honest with you."

"From here on out, it will be difficult for me to believe you," he told her. "Once trust has been broken, it's never easy to rebuild."

"Tell me what I have to do in order for you to trust me again."

"And if I tell you, no matter what it is, you'll agree?"

Mariah inhaled deeply, then exhaled. "Yes."

He heard the reluctance in her voice and knew it hadn't been easy for her to acquiesce. "First, I want you to find out where they're holding Gideon. Then I want you to contact your superiors at the bureau and see what they're doing to find my brother."

"Agreed," she replied quickly.

"That's not all."

She nodded.

"We are not going to escape. Not yet. Not until we know where Gideon is." Jake glanced at the closed door. "We'll fake another hypnosis session and this time you'll report to your Coalition contact that you've made progress breaking down my defenses, that my knowing they have Gideon has made me more cooperative. We have to buy time until either you or the Feds can discover Gideon's location.''

Mariah didn't respond immediately. He could tell she was digesting everything, running it through her logical mind. She could take his offer or leave it— he didn't care. He would never allow her to take him to a safe haven and leave behind his brother and the proof needed to stop the Coalition and their diabolical plans once and for all. He didn't have a death wish—in fact the exact opposite was true—but in the grand scheme of things, his life was insignificant. And on a more personal level, he believed his brother had more to live for than he did. After all, Gideon had a woman who loved him. Jake had none.

''My superiors at the bureau are not going to agree to your demands,'' Mariah said. ''So the best way to deal with them is to make them believe we haven't had the opportunity to escape. Not yet.''

Jake's eyes widened in speculation, understanding what lying to her superiors might mean to Mariah's career, if the truth ever came out. ''You're willing to risk your career to do things my way?''

''If that's what it takes to make you trust me again.'' She met his gaze head-on, without hesitation, unintimidated, equally as strong and determined as he.

''You do have a way to make contact with the bureau, don't you?'' Jake asked.

''Digital phone, in my car,'' she replied. ''I can tell Burgess and Lester that I'm calling my Coalition contact and want some privacy. There's no reason for them not to believe me, if I'm convincing enough. After all neither of them is the sharpest knife in the drawer.''

''Find a way to make both calls—one to your Coalition contact and the other to your FBI contact—as soon as possible. I want to know what you can find out about Gideon from each source. If we're going to save my brother, we need to be armed with as much information as possible.''

Mariah nodded. ''I'm going to uncuff you, but I want you to pretend to be asleep while I'm gone. I'll tell Burgess and Lester that I've given you a couple of injections and it will take about thirty minutes for the drugs to become totally effective. When I come back upstairs, we'll fake a hypnosis session.''

''Make sure those two stay downstairs. We don't want them eavesdropping, do we?''

''I'll put on some music and we'll leave the door open. The music will make it less likely for our voices to carry downstairs and by leaving the door open, we can see them if they get close enough to the door to overhear our conversation.''

Mariah unlocked Jake's handcuffs and for a brief moment they stared at each other. On some basic, male/female level, Jake wanted to trust her, needed to trust her. She'd gotten under his skin in a way no other woman ever had. Sexual desire was a powerful motivator. But he should be thinking with his brain and not another part of his anatomy.

"Go," he told her. "Now."

"Jake...?"

"Not now. Maybe later." He knew she was asking him to discuss forgiving her and trusting her again. But the problem was he didn't know for sure if he could forgive her or trust her, so he couldn't give her a simple yes or no answer. Things between them were far too complicated to see their relationship in black or white, only in shades of gray.

"Lie back and pretend to be asleep," she told him. Her hand hovered near his bloody mouth. "I'm sorry Burgess got rough with you. I should clean your mouth and—"

"No big deal. The blood has dried. Leave it for now. If Burgess notices you've been doctoring me, he won't understand why."

"You're right." She gave him a lingering glance, then turned and headed for the door. "I'll find out what I can."

"Yeah, you do that."

Twenty minutes later, Mariah returned to the upstairs bedroom she shared with Jake. Unfortunately she wasn't alone. Burgess had insisted on helping her set things up for the next hypnosis session and she hadn't protested very strongly, fearing he might become suspicious.

Since she and Jake were not going to attempt an escape anytime soon, she had to maintain her cover, otherwise her life and Jake's would be in imminent danger.

When Burgess and she entered the room, Jake lay quietly on his bed, his eyes closed, his breathing steady and even. Sighing with relief that Jake had followed her instructions to feign sleep, Mariah hurriedly went to work setting the scene, choosing soft, repetitive music that would blend in with conversation and mask the individual words if heard from a distance. She ordered Burgess to adjust the lighting, then once the mood was set, she asked him to help her rouse Jake and get him to his feet.

Jake played his part well, acting lethargic and completely cooperative as they placed him in the chair beside the desk. His arms hung loosely on either side of the chair and his head lolled backward slightly as he seemingly struggled to keep his eyes open.

"Thank you," Mariah told Burgess, offering him a warm smile. "I'll certainly let my boss know how much help you've been to me."

"If he gives you any trouble, just holler." Using his index finger, Burgess tapped Jake in the chest with hard, quick jabs. "You behave yourself, Ingram."

When Burgess went downstairs, leaving the door open behind him, Mariah turned up the music just a bit, then knelt beside Jake and said very softly, "Gideon is alive and safe. For the time being. I won't lie to you ever again. I promise. My Coalition contact informed me that things are beginning to fall apart. They're feeling intense pressure from outside forces and are becoming greatly concerned that Gideon's whereabouts will leak out, so they plan to move him around from one Coalition safe house to another.''

''Damn!''

''Shh. Stay calm. And keep your voice low.''

''Yeah, I understand.''

''More bad news. It will be difficult to find out where Gideon will be at any given time because all info about his location will be transmitted by secret code. His whereabouts within the Coalition will be on a strictly need-to-know basis. And unfortunately, they believe that I don't need to know.''

''Figures.'' Jake glanced at the door. ''What did you tell those two downstairs?''

''The same thing I just told you—the truth.''

''Right.'' Jake focused his attention on Mariah. ''Did you get in touch with your superior at the bureau?''

''Yes, and I shared what information I had with him. They're doing everything they can to find Gideon. And now that they know the info about his whereabouts will be shared in secret code only, they plan to bring in your sister Gretchen to see if she can break the code.''

Jake released an indrawn breath. ''Gretchen is the best. If anyone can break the code, she can. But she'll be under tremendous pressure, knowing that time isn't on our side and Gideon's life might well

be in her hands. And she doesn't need any stress.
Not right now. She's pregnant, you know.''

"Considering the fact that you Extraordinary Five
siblings were only recently reunited and haven't been
together since you were all kids, the loyalty and love
you feel toward one another is remarkable.''

"Each of us is regaining his or her own specific
memories,'' Jake said. "In time we hope to remember everything about the past. It's only natural, considering our sibling bonds go beyond the normal, that
we would reconnect so strongly.''

Mariah heard footsteps. "Shh. I think we're about
to have company again,'' she whispered.

Immediately Jake went into groggy, easily manipulated mode. By the time Lester appeared in the
doorway, the Coalition stooge saw and heard what
he was supposed to—Mariah putting Jake under to
gain control over his subconscious.

"Betty's a lady, and wears a gold ring,'' Mariah
chanted the trigger that Agnes Payne and Olive
Grimble had implanted in Jake's mind when he'd
been a child. "And Johnny's a drummer, who drums
for the king.''

Jake murmured incoherently, pretending the old
conditioning still affected him. Mariah glanced over
her shoulder and glared at Lester. Shaking her head
and placing her index finger to her lips as a signal
for silence, she warned the man off. Lester grinned.
Damn infuriating pest. Go away, she wanted to
shout. If either Lester or Burgess knew anything

about hypnosis other than what they saw on television, neither would buy her act. Lucky for her—and for Jake—that she apparently had the two men fooled.

After several minutes of watching Mariah take Jake deep into a hypnotic trance, Lester came into the room, leaned down and whispered to her, "Can you make him cluck like a chicken?"

Mariah barely contained an exasperated groan. Changing the tone of her voice from the melodic and soothing rhythm she'd been using with Jake to a sharp, no-nonsense clip, she replied in a quiet yet deadly serious manner, "Please leave immediately. You're interfering with my work. You don't want me to report you to—"

"I'm leaving." Lester backed off. "I just thought we might have a little fun with the boy wonder here. Nothing like seeing Mr. Superhuman Genius making a fool of himself."

Mariah simply glowered at Lester, once again amazed that someone hadn't already shot this idiot out of nothing more than sheer aggravation. Lester shrugged, then obediently slithered away.

"Damn little pissant," Mariah said.

Jake reached out and grasped her wrist. "Should I thank you for not making me cluck like a chicken?"

She stared at Jake and couldn't believe he was actually smiling at her. Had his sense of humor returned so quickly? Had he already forgiven her?

"I don't believe any reputable hypnotist would make such an idiotic request of a patient," Mariah said. "But while we're faking these sessions, we should be talking. After all, I'm supposed to be trying to reprogram you. So, I'll ask you some questions and you reply. We need to kill at least an hour before I make a report to my Coalition contact."

"Perhaps we should discuss what you're going to tell him." Jake released her wrist abruptly, as if he had just realized he'd touched something he shouldn't have.

Mariah's breath caught in her throat. She swallowed hard. "All right. What do you suggest? Anything other than you are being cooperative and I seem to have made some progress in reprogramming you, that you're susceptible to the old nursery rhyme trigger?"

"That should be enough…for now." Jake paused, thought awhile, then added, "Maybe you should suggest that it might make me even more cooperative if they brought Gideon here, so that I could see he's all right."

"I don't think they'll buy that argument. They'll want to keep you two apart until they're certain they can control you completely."

Jake nodded. The silence between them became deafening. Mariah rose to her feet and paced around the room. How was she going to do this, be with Jake twenty-four hours a day and not touch him, not act on her feelings? And dammit, she did have feelings—strong feelings—for Jake. Remember you're a federal agent, she told herself. Act like a professional, will you? And not some lovesick teenager!

It shouldn't matter so damn much what Jake thought of her, but it did. As long as she kept him safe, she was doing her job. And if she somehow managed to help him save Gideon and retrieve the all-important computer disks, then Jake would forgive, her, wouldn't he? But by proving her loyalty to Jake, wasn't she also risking the job that meant everything to her? Of course she was.

"Mariah?"

Sensing Jake directly behind her, she gasped, not realizing until that very moment that he'd left the chair and crossed the room. She turned slowly and faced him. Before she had a chance to say anything, he reached out, grabbed her shoulders and pulled her to him.

"I don't trust you," he said, his voice rough.

"I know."

"You lied to me."

"Yes, I did."

"I don't know if I can ever forgive you."

She wanted to cry. And she wanted to swear to him that she'd never betray him ever again. But the words lodged in her throat.

"Damn you, Mariah!"

"Oh, Jake, don't you know that we're both damned."

He shook her once. Tears gathered in the corners of her eyes. He grabbed the nape of her neck and held her in place as his mouth covered hers in a desperate, hungry kiss.

Eight

His mouth ravaged hers, the kiss demanding and turbulent—and tinged with anger. He didn't have to tell her that this savage desire overruled his common sense. She knew only too well, because she felt the same. They were consumed by a hunger bred into their species in primordial times, a basic human instinct. With his lips on hers, his hand grasping her neck, his body pressing intimately, his arousal strong and hard against her, she couldn't resist her own primitive needs. A voice inside her head told her that they shouldn't be doing this. The door was open. They could be seen. And Jake was angry and hurt, the motives for his actions a combination of passion and rage. The logical part of her nature demanded that she put a stop to this immediately; but the emotional side wanted more. Think, dammit, Mariah, think, an inner voice cautioned. But her body disregarded the warning. Her body had needs. Her heart had deep-seated longings.

She clung to him, her hands running wild and free over his shoulders, her fingers threading through his hair. They kissed and touched, their bodies in tune as all five senses came into play. He smelled of soap and water and manliness. Jake's own unique scent. She knew that she could pick him out of a lineup of a dozen men by his scent alone. As he thrust his tongue into her mouth, he moaned, the sound bursting inside her head like skyrockets. Her nipples peaked, her femininity moistened. Ceasing to think coherently, she gave herself over completely to the moment, to feeling and not thinking.

Jake walked her backward, all the while kissing her and touching her. He controlled her, like a puppet on a string. And she didn't care. It didn't matter that she felt powerless to stop him, and completely unable to stop herself. His big hands reached behind her to cup her buttocks and press her against his erection. He kissed her chin and then her throat. One of his hands moved upward, skimming over her hip and waist, reaching higher and higher until he covered one breast and squeezed. Her head lolled back against the wall. Her breasts thrust forward. Jake undid several buttons on her shirt, then lowered his head and put his mouth on her, sucking her through the thin barrier of her cotton bra. Her core throbbed, the need within her escalating quickly. She ached for him.

While she pulsated, her femininity clenching and unclenching, he managed to undo and unzip her slacks. The moment his hand delved into her panties, her thighs parted, giving him easy access to his objective. His fingers worked magic. Rubbing. Stroking. She bit down on her lower lip to keep from crying out, the pleasure was so intense. And when he slipped a couple of fingers inside her, she melted completely. While he manipulated her body to the point of release, they continued kissing feverishly, and in the frenzy Mariah undid his jeans.

Everything happened quickly, at a frenetic pace. Mariah climaxed. And while she trembled with fulfillment, Jake jerked her slacks to her ankles. She kicked them aside, preparing herself for what they both desperately wanted. Jake freed his sex from his briefs, lifted her and rammed himself into her. She clung to him, wild with renewed excitement. He filled her completely, stretching her to her limits. And while he took her, his thrusts hard and deep, only one thought managed to surface through the fog of indescribable pleasure. One word kept repeating itself in her mind. Superhero! Jake was *the* ideal man. Her man.

He came only seconds before she did, so they exploded almost simultaneously . Their breathing labored, sweat glistening on their faces, they stared at each other, really seeing each other for the first time since Jake had kissed her. She noted the satisfaction on his face, the masculine triumph, but she couldn't miss the glimmer of regret in his eyes.

"Mariah, I—"

"No, don't say anything."

He eased out of her, then released her and turned away. She stood against the wall, her knees weak, her body quivering and suddenly realized how vul-

An Important Message from the Editors

Dear Nora Roberts Fan,

Because you've chosen to read one of our wonderful romance novels, we'd like to say "thank you!" And as a special way to thank you, we've selected two books to send you from a series that is similar to the book that you are currently enjoying. Plus, we'll also send an exciting Mystery Gift, absolutely FREE!

Please enjoy them with our compliments.

Pam Powers

Peel off seal and Place inside...

EDITOR'S **FREE GIFT** SEAL
THANK YOU

How to validate your Editor's
FREE GIFT
"Thank You"

1. Peel off gift seal from front cover. Place it in space provided at right. This automatically entitles you to receive 2 FREE BOOKS and a fabulous mystery gift.

2. Send back this card and you'll get 2 brand new novels from Silhouette Romance®, the series that brings you traditional stories of love, marriage and family. These books have a cover price of $3.99 each in the U.S. and $4.50 each in Canada, but they are yours to keep absolutely free.

3. There's no catch. You're under no obligation to buy anything. We charge nothing—ZERO— for your first shipment. And you don't have to make any minimum number of purchases— not even one!

4. The fact is, thousands of readers enjoy receiving their books by mail from the Silhouette Reader Service™. They enjoy the convenience of home delivery...they like getting the best new novels at discount prices BEFORE they're available in stores...and they love their *Heart to Heart* subscriber newsletter featuring author news, horoscopes, recipes, book reviews and much more!

5. We hope that after receiving your free books you'll want to remain a subscriber. But the choice is yours—to continue or cancel, any time at all! So why not take us up on our invitation, with no risk of any kind. You'll be glad you did!

6. And remember...just for validating your Editor's Free Gift Offer, we'll send you THREE gifts, *ABSOLUTELY FREE!*

nerable she was at that very moment. She needed something more from him. A kind word. But she didn't dare allow him to speak, out of fear of what he would say. No kind words. I'm sorry. Or even, You were a good lay, but that's it.

"Is everything all right up there?" Burgess bellowed from downstairs. "I thought I heard some bumping noises? Do you need us, Doc?"

Oh, God! What had she been thinking? That's just it, Mariah, you weren't thinking. Undoubtedly while she and Jake had been going at it like a couple of wild animals, they'd bumped against the wall loud enough to be heard downstairs. Thank goodness neither Burgess nor Lester had come rushing to her rescue. Mariah managed to pull on her slacks and rearrange her clothing hurriedly, despite the need to clean herself and knowing the scent of sex hung heavily on her body. She hurried to the open door and called out a response.

"I'm fine. Mr. Ingram is a little unsteady on his feet and when he got up, he staggered into the wall. I have him under control. But thanks for checking on me."

"Need any help?" Lester chimed in.

"No, thank you!"

Mariah closed the door, then forced herself to turn and face Jake. His shirt still hung open, but he'd zipped his jeans. He looked like someone who'd just had sex—and enjoyed it. No doubt she had the same look.

"We took a stupid risk," she said. "I can't believe we did that."

His expression somber, Jake replied, "What just happened doesn't really change things. I still don't trust you."

She nodded.

"I don't trust you and I haven't forgiven you for lying to me, but I wanted you so much I couldn't think straight," he told her. "You've got my mind and my emotions all screwed up, and I hate like hell to admit that to you. But I'm not going to lie to you. I consider whatever happens between us to be nothing more than temporary insanity. Do you understand?"

Oh, yes, she understood, all right. He wanted to have sex with her, but he didn't really want her. No commitments. No love. No affair of the heart. It was nothing more to him than you-scratch-my-itch-I'll-scratch-yours. This was a first for her—sex for the sake of sex. No emotional ties. She'd never had sex with a man she didn't care for deeply.

Get real, Mariah, you care about Jake. You care too damn much. You have an emotional investment in him. But she couldn't kid herself about Jake's feelings. He'd made them perfectly clear.

"Mariah? Do you understand?" he repeated the question, apparently needing a verbal response.

"Yes, I understand. We just had sex. And if it happens again, that's all it will be. Sex. Nothing more. I get it. You don't have to tell me again."

"You say you understand, but you sound upset. Are you sure—"

"I'm a big girl, Jake. I'm not some simpering teenage virgin who believes you love me. We've got the hots for each other. Anything this hot will burn itself out pretty fast."

"Right. Sexual attraction combined with close proximity equals—"

"Mutual stupidity."

That comment gained her a tentative smile from Jake. He ran his hand over his mouth and jaw. "We're damn lucky we didn't get caught in the act."

"Uh-huh. Next time, we'll be more careful."

Jake cocked his head to one side and gave her an inquisitive glance. "Next time?"

Mariah sighed. Oh, great, she thought. Open mouth, insert foot. "Yes, next time. And we both know there will be a next time. This hot thing between us can't burn itself out without adding more fuel to the flames."

"I like the way you think." He cleared his throat, apparently in an effort not to laugh. "Most women wouldn't look at our situation the way you have."

"I'm not most women. Or haven't you already figured that out?"

"I'm beginning to," he told her. "I'm beginning to."

Switching gears while she was still ahead, Mariah said, "I'm going to clean up in the bathroom. Stay here and stay quiet. When I finish, the bathroom is all yours. I'll go downstairs and give my comrades a positive report on our second hypnosis session."

"I assume you're going to let them know we'll be undertaking another session this afternoon and you'll want complete privacy."

Mariah's heart skipped a beat. She knew what Jake was asking. Sex in the afternoon.

"Of course, we'll need another session. There's no need not to enjoy ourselves while we're playing this game."

With that said, she left him alone and escaped into the bathroom. After she freshened up, she looked at herself in the mirror.

"You're a fool, Mariah," she told herself aloud. "A damn fool. You're going to wind up with a broken heart." And since Jake doesn't have any condoms, you just might wind up pregnant. Oh, God! She groaned. Yeah, that little thought never crossed your mind, did it?

For all she knew, she could have already conceived Jake's child. And what bothered her more than anything was the fact that she wasn't overly concerned, wasn't even upset at the thought of being pregnant.

Needing to put some space between them, Mariah deliberately stayed away from Jake until after lunch. She'd fed Burgess and Lester a line of bull. Thankfully they had believed her without question. Lester had, as usual, made a pest of himself, but nothing she couldn't handle. And when she had requested that Burgess take lunch upstairs to Jake as a reward for Jake's cooperation, he'd spared her having to face her lover until later. Despite wanting to be alone with Jake, she suspected that the wise thing to do was have Burgess hang around while she faked another session later today. The more she had sex with Jake, the more likely it was that she'd fall deeper in love with him.

Mariah jumped up off the sofa. "I'm going to take a walk. I need some fresh air and I should report in."

"Need some company?" Lester asked.

Mariah simply gave him an eat-dirt-and-die glance.

"You'd better wrap up good," Lester told her. "It's colder than a witch's—"

"Don't follow me," she warned him. "I'll have my pistol with me and I'd just love for you to give me a reason to use it on you. I want a little privacy when I make my call. My reports to headquarters are none of your business."

Burgess chuckled. Lester snapped his head around and glowered at his partner. Mariah took that opportunity to escape the aggravating twosome. She slipped into her down jacket and pulled her knitted cap over her head, but didn't remove the gloves stuffed into her coat pocket. After exiting through the kitchen door and entering the garage, she went directly to her vehicle, unlocked it and slid into the driver's seat. After retrieving her cell phone, she punched in the number for her Coalition contact and waited, tapping her fingers against the steering wheel. He answered on the fifth ring.

"I have good news," she said. "Mr. Ingram co-operated fully, if somewhat reluctantly, during this morning's session. I believe I'll be able to reprogram him, but it's going to take time. Even though he's willing to cooperate in the hopes of saving his brother, his subconscious mind is resisting."

"We're willing to give you more time, but there is a limit to how long we'll wait."

"If Mr. Ingram could see his brother—"

"Not possible. I thought I made that clear to you."

"Yes, you did." Mariah decided it would be use-less to pursue the matter. She knew she couldn't come up with a persuasive argument, which meant they would have to find a way to locate Gideon. "I'll call tomorrow with another update."

With that conversation ended, she got out of the TrailBlazer, punched in the number for her FBI contact, then slipped on her gloves and walked outside into the frigid afternoon. A north wind whipped around her, slicing through the barrier of her thick winter clothes, pinking her cheeks and nose, and va-porizing her warm breath.

When she heard the agent's voice on the other end of the line, she said, "Ingram refuses to come with me. He's determined to find his brother. I need to know where they're holding Gideon Faulkner so I can promise Jake our guys will be able to rescue him.''

"Good news and bad news," the agent told her.

Mariah groaned. "Hit me with it."

"Gretchen Miller broke the secret code the Coalition has been using."

"Hallelujah. So this means—" She stopped herself abruptly. "That was the good news, wasn't it? So what's the bad news?"

"We went in after Faulkner, but came up empty-handed. The Coalition had already moved Ingram's brother and now they know we've broken the code, so…"

"So, they won't use that code anymore." Great. just great, Mariah thought. One step forward, two steps back. It would make things easier if she didn't tell Jake about this. But she'd learned her lesson. No more lies between them. No more secrets.

"Look, Daley, if you can't get Ingram to agree to leave with you, then use whatever means necessary to get him to us. Understand?"

"Yes, I understand." Drug Jake. Knock him out. Bring him in. Make sure he's safe. "It could take days before another opportunity to escape arises."

"When it does, take it. Don't hesitate. And do not allow Ingram's determination to save his brother influence you in any way."

"Yes, sir."

Mariah punched the off button on the phone and

returned it to her coat pocket. She'd already walked down the gravel road about a quarter of a mile. She picked up her pace to a slow jog as her mind absorbed all the information. Her loyalty lay with the bureau. Her future depended upon her doing this job well, and that meant following orders. But if she followed orders, she'd have to betray Jake.

Make a decision, she told herself. Make a decision and stick to it. Are you willing to risk your career to prove your loyalty to Jake? Breathing in the cold, crisp air, she broke into a run, filling her lungs, testing her fitness. But no matter how hard she tried, she could not outrun her problems. Mariah stopped, bent over and caught her breath, allowing her body to rest and her heartbeat to slow. She was a federal agent working undercover, which meant playing a part, deceiving the bad guys, making them believe she was one of them. And if she stood by Jake in this matter that would mean deceiving her own team, lying to them in order to allow Jake to handle his brother's kidnapping in his own way.

So, what's it going to be Mariah—Jake or your career? She'd worked her whole life to reach this point in her career, to achieve a position that her brothers envied and her father greatly respected. She was damn good at her job and her future with the bureau looked bright. On the other hand, what did she have with Jake? Sexual chemistry? They had no past and no future. She didn't mean anything more to him than a warm body. They were simply two ships passing in the night.

Mariah knew what she had to do. It was just a matter of doing it.

Jake had wolfed down lunch, then alternated between pacing the floor and lying in bed staring up at the ceiling. The hours alone had given him too much time to think. About Gideon. About his own situation. And about Mariah. He knew what he had to do. He had to find his brother and rescue him, with or without Mariah's help. His first allegiance was to his new family. Protecting them had to be his main focus. Mariah was a distraction he didn't need. He couldn't believe he'd had unprotected sex with her. That alone proved her hold over him. He'd never done anything that stupid in his entire life. Saving his brother wasn't simply an act of brotherly concern. Gideon's capture could result in another international crime with dire, far-reaching consequences. If forced to participate in further criminal acts, Gideon might never recover emotionally. And once his usefulness ended, the Coalition would dispose of him like yesterday's trash.

Jake knew that if he allowed himself to care about Mariah, she would become a liability. The Coalition was already using his devotion to his brother in the hopes of controlling him. If they ever discovered that he had deep feelings for Mariah, her life would be endangered. He couldn't allow that to happen.

But do you have deep feelings for her? Jake asked himself. Yeah, sure, you feel something for her. But are those feelings coming from your heart…or from the southern regions of your anatomy? Wanting to have sex with a woman and loving a woman were often two separate desires. The two had been combined in his relationship with Tara, but he hadn't hungered for Tara the way he did Mariah. Face it, hotshot, you might not be in love with your FBI bodyguard, but you'd do just about anything to protect her, just as you would to protect your family. Doesn't that tell you anything?

The sound of footsteps on the stairs alerted him that he'd soon have company, and from the lightness of the taps, he suspected it was Mariah. He sat up and dropped his feet to the floor, then looked toward the open door. She paused before entering, as if waiting for his permission.

"I'd begun to think you'd run off and left me," he said, halfway joking. But he couldn't completely erase a niggling uncertainty. As with many adopted children, Jake had had abandonment issues that he'd worked through years ago, and then he'd met Violet Vaughn and learned the truth about his personal history. Still reeling from that discovery, he'd been dealt another emotional blow when Tara had ended their engagement. He was better off without Tara and he knew it, but being rejected by someone you thought you'd spend the rest of your life with certainly made a man question any other woman's loyalty.

"I'm not leaving here without you," Mariah told him as she walked into the bedroom they shared. "Until this situation ends in a satisfactory resolution for everyone concerned—you, Gideon, me and the bureau—you and I are going to be joined at the hip, so to speak."

Jake grinned. "I'd rather we be joined at another location other than the hip."

Her lips twitched. "That can be arranged."

"You were gone an awfully long time." Jake stood up beside the bed. "What have you been doing, playing footsies with Burgess and Lester?"

"Ha-ha."

"Not for Lester's lack of trying, I'm sure."

"Jealous?"

Jake chuckled. "Not of Lester, since I know how you loathe him. But, to be honest, I would be jealous of any other man. I tend to be the possessive type."

She stared at him, apparently speechless.

"No clever response. If you can't think fast on your feet, you'll never checkmate me."

Mariah sighed. "I think that the best I could hope for with you would be a tie. There are ties in chess, right?"

"A draw," he told her. "If the players choose not to continue a game they can agree to a draw."

"But we haven't reached that point, have we? We both still want to play."

"I don't see us willingly stopping the game. We'll play until one of us checkmates the other. You know, someday I'll have to teach you to play chess. I believe you'd make a formidable opponent.''

She walked toward him. He waited for her, realizing he wanted her to make the first move. When she was only a couple of feet away, she paused and looked directly into his eyes.

''As much as I enjoy our witty repartée, we need to get serious. I have something to tell you,'' Mariah said.

''Something serious by the tone of your voice.''

''Your sister Gretchen broke the Coalition's secret code. No, don't get excited. Agents were assigned to raid the location where Gideon was being held. Unfortunately, they'd already moved your brother by the time our agents showed up.''

''Don't tell me—the Coalition has now changed their code, so we're back to square one.''

''Not quite.''

He studied her speculatively.

''I've been given orders to bring you in,'' she told him.

''You know I won't go. Not until we've freed Gideon.''

''Yes, I know. But my orders are to bring you in, one way or another.''

''I see.''

''No, Jake, that's just it—you don't see.''

''Meaning?''

''Meaning I had to make a decision about which is more important to me—my career with the bureau or my relationship with you.''

Nine

Jake stared at Mariah, every nerve in his body at full alert, his muscles tense, as he waited for her to say the words he dreaded. He should have realized that she would be forced to choose between her career and him. Of course she would choose her career. What other choice did she have? After all, despite the strong physical attraction between them, they were little more than strangers.

"You do what you have to do," Jake told her. "But don't think that I'll make it easy for you to take me in."

Mariah gazed at him, her vision clear, not muddled with feminine tears. He supposed it took an unemotional type of female to be a federal agent, someone able to do a difficult job without falling apart.

"I'm not going to take you in," she said. "I plan to do all I can to help you find Gideon and rescue him."

Jake squinted, narrowing his gaze. "Are you actually saying that you—"

"That I've chosen loyalty to you over dedication to my career."

"But why? I don't understand. You've said yourself that what's between us is just sex. You don't love me…'' Jake's voice failed as he saw the truth in her expression. My God! She did love him. Or at least she believed she did. And she was willing to put her career on the line for his sake.

So, how does that make you feel? he asked himself.

About ten feet tall.

"We don't need to discuss it," Mariah said. "I mean…if it makes you uncomfortable. And I'm not sure exactly what to call it. Love? Maybe. I don't know. All I know is that I can't—I won't—betray you. And every instinct I have is telling me that the most important thing in my life right now is helping you.''

"I'm surprised, to say the least.''

"Why? Didn't you suspect how I felt?''

"It's a two-way thing, you know. I feel something for you, too. Something stronger than simple sexual attraction.''

"Sexual attraction is seldom simple," she said. "Especially not for people like us.''

Jake grinned. "You've got that right.''

"Look, I think we should fake another session in the morning. Afterward, I'll call my contact and tell him we're making progress and I'll see if I can find out anything new about Gideon.''

Jake reached out and caressed Mariah's cheek. "We need to buy more time, enough so that your people can find Gideon.'' Jake slid his hand down to her shoulder. "No matter what happens, I'll never forget what you're doing for me. When this is all over—"

"No!" Mariah shook her head. "We can't know what the future holds, so let's not make any promises that we might not be able to keep. For now, we're a team. Later, we'll see."

"A very sensible approach to a rather sensitive subject."

"Believe it or not, I usually tend to be very sensible."

"I believe it," he told her. "I don't usually allow anything other than logic to dictate my actions, but lately…"

"Lately we've both been acting out of character."

"Are you saying we bring out the worst in each other?"

Mariah shrugged. "Who knows? Maybe it's the other way around. Maybe we bring out the best in each other. Loyalty, understanding, sympathy and even love, at least some sort of love."

"You're the only woman I've ever known who doesn't brandish that word about as if it was a cure-all for every problem." He squeezed her shoulder, then released his hold. "Saying I love you should mean something important. It should never be said lightly."

"For once we're in complete agreement."

"Friends and partners?" Jake held out his hand.

Mariah stared at his hand for a couple of seconds

before clasping it. "Friends and partners." They shook hands.

"And lovers," Jake added, still holding her hand.

"Lovers." She whispered the word softly, then slipped her hand from his.

Jake suspected that any vulnerability Mariah might feel, she would hide from him. For a strong, independent woman, with a competitive nature, Mariah must have found it difficult to admit to him that she was willing to risk her career to prove herself to him. Some might see that as a weakness—a woman willing to sacrifice everything for a man. But he actually saw it as a strength, and admired Mariah all the more. And to be completely honest, it deepened his feelings for her. But he couldn't—wouldn't—look too closely at those feelings. Now was not the time to figure out why Mariah Daley was like no other woman he'd ever known or why he felt a connection with her that surpassed anything else. Even his link to his biological siblings? If it came to a showdown, if he had to choose between his siblings and Mariah, what choice would he make?

"You know that saving Gideon is my top priority," Jake said.

Mariah nodded. "I know. And I understand. I happen to have three big brothers and I'd do just about anything for them."

"Is that one of the reasons you decided to help me?"

"That and the obvious." A fragile smile lifted the corners of her mouth.

"I'd hate to see you wind up in trouble because of me."

"Too late. I'm already in trouble. Actually, I'm in way over my head. Being totally crazy about a guy is not something I've experienced before and I haven't handled things the way I should have."

Jake could not allow himself the luxury of caring too deeply for Mariah, not when his life was so complicated. He needed to focus all his attention on rescuing his brother and retrieving the computer disks. Sorting through his feelings for Mariah was a distraction he couldn't afford.

And last but not least, he couldn't be sure he'd come out of this situation alive. For all he knew he was already living on borrowed time.

"The way I see it, you're handling things a damn sight better than I am." Jake wanted to pull Mariah into his arms, hold her, kiss her, comfort her. He wanted to promise her a future for the two of them together.

Drawn to each other, unable to resist the sexual and emotional magnetism that bound them, Mariah and Jake came together in the middle of the room. Standing there, not touching, only looking into each other's eyes, they shared a silent moment of complete understanding. Words were superfluous.

Booted footsteps echoed up the staircase. Mariah jerked backward, away from Jake. He rushed toward the bed and sat down on the edge, then bowed his head and stared at the floor. A couple of minutes later, Burgess paused in the doorway. Mariah turned to greet him.

"Is something wrong?" she asked.

"Phone call for you," Burgess replied.

"I'll be right down." She turned to Jake. "Manacling you to the bedpost won't be necessary, will it?"

Jake looked up at her without lifting his head. "No, it won't be necessary."

"Are you planning another session this evening?" Burgess asked.

"No. I've postponed the next session until tomorrow morning."

Mariah turned around and walked out into the hall, directly past Burgess, who quickly fell into step beside her. Jake waited until he was certain they'd reached the bottom of the stairs before he moved. He paced the floor quietly, wondering what Mariah's phone call was about, and if it had anything to do with Gideon.

Mariah picked up the receiver where Burgess had placed it on the table. "Mariah Brooks here," she said.

"Dr. Brooks, we're delighted that you're making progress with Jake."

The feminine voice sounded familiar. Mariah was certain she'd heard it before, but where and when?

"He's definitely been more cooperative since learning about his brother's capture."

Before she figured out her caller's identity, the woman spoke again. "Oliver and I are eager to see firsthand just how much you've been able to accomplish with our number-one wonder boy."

Oliver? God help her, she was talking to Agnes Payne, the she-demon who was the true mastermind of the Coalition. Everyone within the organization knew that Agnes simply allowed Willard Croft to believe he was running the show. A malevolent ruthlessness dominated Ms. Payne's personality, and her true soul mate, Oliver Grimble, had been paired with her in marriage and treachery for over thirty years.

"You want to see Jake?" Mariah asked.

"Yes, of course we do."

"When? If you'll give me another week—"

"Nonsense. A week is far too long."

"A few more days, then."

"Not even a few hours," Agnes said.

"What?"

"Oliver and I are on our way to the cabin as we speak. We should be on your doorstep within five minutes."

Five minutes! That wasn't nearly enough time to prepare Jake. If Dr. Grimble and Dr. Payne examined Jake, they would realize soon enough that he hadn't been reprogrammed, that everything she'd been telling her Coalition contact had been a lie. Dear God, what was she going to do?

Stay calm, she told herself.

"I look forward to seeing you again, Dr. Payne," Mariah said. "You probably don't remember our first meeting several months ago."

"Of course I remember," Agnes replied. "When you volunteered for the job of reprogramming Jake, I personally okayed you for the assignment. Now I'm quite eager to see your handiwork."

"The reprogramming is not complete. We've only begun to make progress."

"I understand, but now that Jake is cooperating, it shouldn't take Oliver long to complete the job you've begun. He's quite good at this sort of thing."

"Yes, so I understand." Get off the phone, Mariah told herself. Go upstairs and warn Jake. "I should go now and prepare Jake for your arrival."

"No! Don't tell him. I want it to be a surprise."

"Oh. All right."

Adrenaline pumped through Mariah's system at a maddening pace. They were in trouble. Big trouble. And she had only a few minutes to think of a way to save them.

But how could she think when Agnes Payne insisted on continuing their conversation? She kept trying to get off the phone, but the woman didn't stop talking until Mariah heard Agnes and Oliver's vehicle pull up in the driveway. Damn! They were screwed!

"We've arrived," Agnes said. "Put on some coffee and we'll talk in person."

Bracing herself to face the devil and her obedient husband, Mariah hung up the phone, squared her shoulders and turned to Burgess. "Agnes Payne and Oliver Grimble are here to see Jake Ingram. Please, go outside and meet them and make sure you show them the proper respect. You do know who they are, don't you?"

"Yeah, I know," Burgess said. "They're a couple of high muckety-mucks in the Coalition."

Lester stuck his head around the corner of the kitchen door. "Want me to go with Burgess or should I run upstairs and bring supergenius down here?"

"Neither." Mariah shooed Burgess with her hand and he immediately headed for the front door. "You are to behave and be quiet. Don't say anything unless you're spoken to. Is that understood?"

Stay calm, Mariah cautioned herself once again. Don't panic. Not yet. If only she'd had a couple of hours to prepare Jake, to walk him through some sort of playacting. Or if she'd had more warning—say overnight—she might have been able to persuade Jake to escape. But she didn't have overnight or even a couple of hours. She had minutes.

Agnes Payne entered the house first. A small woman, almost petite, in her early sixties, with keen brown eyes and a halo of curly dark hair barely touched by gray, she exuded an aura of power, intelligence and evil. A man of about 5' 10", with thick gray hair and tired blue eyes, came into the room following his mate like a dutiful dog, his shoulders slightly slumped as if he carried the weight of the world on them. Although Mariah knew from the report she'd read on Grimble that he was several years younger than Agnes, tonight he looked older. At one glance it was easy to see who the dominant partner was in their relationship. Mariah had no doubt that without his wife, Oliver Grimble would be totally lost.

"Dr. Brooks." Agnes held out her hand.

Mariah exchanged a strong, quick shake with the other woman. "Dr. Payne."

"Where is Jake?" Agnes asked.

"He's upstairs," Mariah answered.

Oliver Grimble glanced around, noting that both Burgess and Lester were in the room. "You've left Jake unguarded?"

"He's quite safe and secure," Mariah assured them. "There are bars on the upstairs windows and no means of escape."

"Yes, of course." Agnes turned to her husband. "My dear, I know you'd like to be the first to take a look at what Dr. Brooks has accomplished with our Jake, so why don't you go on upstairs and have a talk with him. I'll be up shortly." Agnes removed her coat and handed it to Mariah, then pointed to Burgess. "You go with Dr. Grimble."

"Perhaps I should go," Mariah said, clutching Agnes's coat. "After all, I'm the one who has worked with Jake and the person he'd feel most comfortable with at this point."

"I've promised Oliver a few moments with Jake without any interference." Agnes patted Mariah's arm. "It's frightfully cold outside and I'm quite chilled. Why don't we share a cup of coffee and you can explain the methods you've used that have worked successfully."

Mariah's fake smile made her face ache, but she kept it in place by sheer force of will. All she could do now was pray, because it was going to take a miracle to save them. "I'm afraid I didn't have time to put on coffee, but if you'll come with me into the kitchen, it won't take long to prepare a fresh pot." Mariah laid Agnes's coat on a nearby chair.

As she escorted Agnes into the kitchen, Mariah glanced over her shoulder in time to see Burgess following Oliver up the stairs. How would Jake react when he saw the man who had brainwashed him when he'd been a child? And more importantly, what would Dr. Grimble do when he discovered that she had made absolutely no progress at reprogramming Jake?

While the coffee brewed, Mariah racked her brain for every ounce of knowledge she'd gained in her college psychology courses, hoping her responses to Agnes's questions seemed genuine. As the minutes passed, Mariah tried not to glance at her wristwatch or the clock on the stove. Thankfully, at the moment,

Agnes seemed more interested in enjoying the fresh, hot coffee than anything else.

"Would you care for something to eat?" Mariah asked.

"No, thank you." Agnes lifted the coffee mug to her lips again.

"I really think I should go upstairs and help Dr. Grimble. Jake might respond better if—"

"You seem awfully nervous, Dr. Brooks."

"I am nervous. I'm concerned about Jake, about how he might react to Dr. Grimble. He was totally uncooperative at first and downright hostile."

"Until he was told that we now have Gideon back with us."

"Yes, until he learned his brother had been captured."

"I realize that you might feel proprietorial where Jake is concerned and consider yourself his doctor, but must I remind you that Oliver was the person who programmed Jake and his siblings. If you've done your job and conditioned Jake correctly, then Oliver should have no trouble in making quick progress with him."

"Jake could react violently when he sees Dr. Grimble."

"Yes, he could. That's why I sent Burgess with Ollie."

Mariah realized that all the talk in the world was not going to change anything. Perhaps she should consider another alternative. Was there any way she could get the upper hand in this situation? Could she take on Agnes and Oliver, as well as Burgess and Lester? No, she couldn't. If she tried to play the hero, she could easily get Jake killed, not to mention herself, too.

The minutes dragged by, each second like an hour. Mariah finally gave in to temptation and glanced at the clock on the stove. Damn! Oliver Grimble had been upstairs with Jake for nearly twenty minutes, while she'd been faking a hundred and one answers to Agnes Payne's endless questions. Once or twice Agnes had cocked an eyebrow as if some of Mariah's responses had surprised her, so Mariah had no idea if she had convinced the woman that she actually knew what she was talking about.

Suddenly the kitchen door burst open and Burgess shoved Jake into the room. Jake, who was now handcuffed, hazarded a quick glance in Mariah's direction and when their gazes met, she read the bad news in Jake's eyes.

Oliver Grimble marched into the room and pointed a condemning finger at Jake. ''He's useless to us as he is now.'' Grimble glowered at Mariah. ''I don't know what she's been doing with Jake, but she has made absolutely no progress in conditioning him for reprogramming.''

Agnes snapped her head around and her beady-eyed gaze raked over Mariah. ''You've been lying to us, Dr. Brooks.''

''No, I haven't been lying. I truly believed that I'd

made progress with him. He seemed receptive. He—''

Agnes slapped her open palm down on the table. The sound reverberated throughout the kitchen. ''Stop lying! You've failed at your first important assignment for us. And I'm asking myself why.''

''I got a good answer to that one.'' Lester came out of the shadows.

Agnes focused on the loathsome creature. ''And you're…?''

''Lester. And I know why Dr. Brooks didn't do what she was supposed to do to Mr. Genius IQ.''

''And just what is your theory, Lester?'' Agnes asked.

''She's got the hots for him. My guess is that instead of brainwashing him, she's been messing around with him. If you know what I mean.''

Agnes turned her wicked glare on Mariah. ''Is that true? Have you fallen in love with our Jake?'' Agnes walked across the room to where Burgess stood guard over a subdued Jake. She reached out and ran her fingertips over Jake's cheek. He recoiled as if her touch had poisoned him. ''He is quite beautiful, isn't he? The ideal man.''

''Lester's crazy,'' Mariah said. ''He's angry with me because I rebuffed his crude advances.''

''Whatever her reasons, Dr. Brooks has done nothing to condition Jake,'' Oliver said. ''We've wasted time—wasted days—depending on her to prepare him. I'll be starting at square one and from what I've

seen of him tonight, I'm not sure Jake can be reprogrammed.''

Agnes clutched Jake's chin. ''If you don't cooperate with us, we will kill Gideon. I'd hate to lose
him because I believe he can be useful to us again
in the future, but the choice is yours. Your brother's
life is in your hands.''

''I want Gideon set free,'' Jake said, his voice
terse, his jaw clenched.

''In exchange for?'' Agnes asked.

''My full cooperation.''

A deep sigh died inside Mariah as she tightened
her lips to prevent its escape. No, Jake, don't do this,
she wanted to scream. Don't sacrifice yourself! I
can't bear it if I lose you.

Ten

"An interesting proposition," Agnes said as she studied Jake, who held his head high and looked his enemy right in the eye. "I'm curious as to why you didn't make this offer to Dr. Brooks—" Agnes shot a sidelong glance at Mariah "—unless of course you thought you could manipulate her. Is that what happened? You used your charm to persuade her that she means something to you in order to use her to your advantage?"

"Dr. Brooks is a flunky, much like Burgess and Lester," Jake said. "I don't deal with underlings. I outsmart them. And that's what I did with Dr. Brooks. I simply outsmarted her, made her believe that I was succumbing to her hypnosis techniques."

"Is that what you want me to believe?" Agnes smiled.

Agnes's sinister grin sent cold chills up Mariah's spine. The woman suspected Mariah was not on the up-and-up. It was only a matter of time before she found out the truth—that Mariah wasn't a psychiatrist dedicated to the Coalition, that she was a federal agent who had infiltrated the organization.

"If I were to believe that, I'd have to assume that

Dr. Brooks is totally incompetent and her credentials are fraudulent.'' Agnes got right up in Jake's face. "That's it, isn't it? Our Dr. Brooks is a fraud."

"I have no idea who or what she is," Jake replied. "For all I know she's Minnie Mouse in disguise. I'm telling you that she sure as hell had me fooled. She certainly conducted herself the way a Coalition psychiatrist would. It isn't her fault that I'm not susceptible to mind control."

"He's lying," Lester chimed in, his gaze darting back and forth from Agnes to Mariah. "She treated him way too good from the very beginning. She coddled him, that's what she did."

Agnes pinned Burgess with her stare. "Is he right? Did Dr. Brooks treat Jake with kid gloves?"

"Yes, ma'am. In the beginning. But when those tactics didn't work, she started getting tougher with him."

Agnes contemplated the situation. Mariah could practically see the wheels in her head turning. She knew the woman was smart—too smart not to put two and two together and come up with the obvious four.

"I'm not sure what to believe at this point," Agnes admitted. "I need time to think." She turned to her husband. "We need to talk. Privately." Oliver nodded. Agnes then looked at Burgess. "Take Jake and Dr. Brooks upstairs and lock them in for the time being. I want you or Lester guarding the door at all times until I decide what we're going to do." Agnes surveyed Mariah from head to toe. "Remove Dr. Brooks's gun. She's not going to be needing it."

Mariah didn't protest—how could she?—when Burgess followed Agnes Payne's orders and took the Smith & Wesson from her hip holster.

"Make it easy on yourself," Jake said. "Let me see my brother, assure myself that he's all right, then when you release him, I'm all yours."

"That does seem an easy solution." Agnes laid her hand on Mariah's shoulder. "But it doesn't solve our problem with Dr. Brooks. She's a puzzle I intend to solve."

"Dr. Brooks has nothing to do with it," Jake told Agnes. "I told you that I fooled her. You can't judge her abilities as a psychiatrist by whether or not she was able to condition me for reprogramming."

"Perhaps you're right, but I don't intend to make any hasty decisions—about you or Dr. Brooks." With a flick of her hand Agnes motioned for Burgess to remove Jake and Mariah.

Both she and Jake cooperated. After all, what other choice did they have right now? Once upstairs, locked in and alone, they might be able to put their heads together and come up with a plan. Mariah led the trek, with Jake behind her and both Burgess and Lester trailing them. She despised Lester all the more now because he was enjoying her predicament far too much. It was only a matter of time before he tried something with her now that he knew he didn't have to take orders from her.

"Get inside," Burgess instructed when they reached the bedroom.

Mariah rushed inside, but before Jake could follow, Burgess gave him a hard shove that sent him crashing into the room and onto his knees. Lester, who had followed them upstairs, laughed like the braying jackass he was. Burgess slammed the door shut and locked it. Mariah rushed to Jake, but he put up his hand in a back-off warning. He lifted himself to his feet, then standing straight and tall, he glared at the closed door. Glancing at Mariah, he put a finger to his lips to indicate silence. She nodded. After she moved across the room to the point farthest from the door, she motioned for Jake to come to her. He joined her immediately. They hovered in the corner near the closet.

"It's only a matter of time before they move us," she whispered. "I have to act quickly." Mariah balanced herself by placing a hand on Jake's shoulder, then she crossed her leg and lifted her booted foot upward.

"What the hell are you doing?" Jake asked, keeping his voice low.

"I've got a micro-transmitter hidden in the heel of my boot. It's for emergency use only. If I send a signal, federal agents will surround this place within a couple of hours."

"Why haven't you used it before?"

"Because the goal of my mission was to keep you safe, at all costs, even my own life. I couldn't risk

Burgess or Lester killing you if we were stormed by federal agents. But now that my cover is all but blown and you've decided that our only way out is to sacrifice yourself, we have nothing to lose, do we?''

"What about Gideon?''

"If you make a deal with Agnes and Oliver, you have no guarantee they'll keep their end of the bargain. My bet is they'll keep both you and Gideon. A deal with them is a deal with the devil.''

"Don't send the transmission.'' Jake grabbed her hand. "Please.''

Mariah knew that Jake wasn't a man who begged. Not ever. He wasn't the type who'd asked favors or depend on others. But he'd said please. And she could see by the look in his eyes that he was pleading with her.

"Sending the signal could be our only chance of survival,'' Mariah told him. "Is Gideon's life worth more to you than your own?'' Is his life worth more to you than mine?

"As long as we're alive and cooperative, we've got a chance. But Gideon has no chance. And he's got Brooke. So whose life is more important?''

Yours. Your life is more important to me. But she understood Jake's reasoning. If it were one of her brothers, she'd exchange her life for his with few second thoughts.

Mariah snapped the boot heel back in place, lowered her foot to the floor and looked directly at Jake. "Is there a Plan B?"

Jake grinned. "That's my girl." He skimmed her cheek with the back of his hand. "Plan B is to cooperate with the enemy—up to a point."

"Up to what point?"

"Up to the point where they free Gideon and you," Jake told her. He halted her protest. "I've got to get you out of here. Agnes is downstairs right now putting everything together. Now that you're under suspicion, she'll do whatever she has to do to find out what you're all about. And once she knows you're a fed—"

"I'll be as good as dead."

He grasped her shoulders and shook her gently. "I'm not going to let that happen. The first opportunity you get to leave, I want you to go and not look back."

"Do you expect me to leave you, to let them—"

He silenced her with a kiss. Quick, tender and totally effective. When he lifted his head, she simply stared at him. Quiet. Pensive. She realized it would be no use to argue the point with him. Jake had made up his mind to sacrifice himself to save Gideon—and to save her. What he didn't know was that she wasn't the type to accept his noble sacrifice, at least not for her. Either Jake and she came out of this together or not at all. He wasn't the only one willing to put his life on the line for the people he loved.

"Jake...no matter what happens, I want you to know something."

He stared at her quizzically.

"I'm glad we've had this time together, despite the circumstances."

"Yeah, me, too."

Mariah slipped away from him and walked over to the window, raised the blinds and stared up at the dark night sky. If only there weren't any bars on the windows. If only Agnes and Oliver hadn't shown up when they did. If only—

Jake came up behind her, slid his arms around her and pulled her back against him. He nuzzled the side of her neck and whispered her name. "Mariah. My wonderful Mariah."

Less than an hour later, Burgess unlocked the door and he and Lester stormed into the room. Burgess handcuffed Jake and herded him out of the bedroom. A leering Lester grabbed Mariah's arm and dragged her toward the door.

"I'm in charge of you now." Lester's broad grin revealed his crooked, yellow teeth.

Mariah swallowed hard. A tight knot of apprehension formed in the pit of her stomach. She hated having him touch her. He took such perverse pleasure in their reversed circumstances.

When the four of them reached the living room, Agnes was nowhere to be seen. Oliver issued the orders. "Cuff her, too. We want her treated as a prisoner for the time being. Put them in your vehicle and follow closely behind us. We're moving them to another position tonight. Somewhere we know they'll be secure. We're too close to getting what we want to take any chances.''

Mariah stole a quick glance in Jake's direction and she knew he was thinking the same thing she was— that it wouldn't have mattered if she'd sent the SOS earlier. By the time the Feds could have gotten here, they'd have been long gone.

Neither Mariah nor Jake put up a fuss when Burgess and Lester escorted them to the Saturn SUV. Now was not the time to try for an escape. But Mariah would be waiting and watching for an opportunity, one less risky than the present situation.

Burgess opened the side door and shoved Jake inside, then he opened the passenger door, reached inside the glove compartment of the SUV and pulled out a pair of handcuffs. After tossing them to Lester, he said, ''Cuff her, then toss her in the back with Ingram. You'll have to keep an eye on them while I drive. We don't want any screwups.''

Lester eagerly manacled her wrists, then jerked her back so that he could easily whisper in her ear. ''Just think of the fun we'll have later. You with your hands bound behind your back and my hands all over you.''

Mariah glared at him. He laughed, then kissed her neck. She quivered with revulsion. When he yanked her around to face him, he grabbed her face with one hand. She knew he intended to kiss her on the mouth. Acting on pure instinct, she spit in his face. He stopped dead still, shock and anger etching his features.

He reached up and wiped the spittle from his face with his palm, then wiped his hand on his jeans. "A regular little spitfire, aren't you? That don't bother me none. All the more fun for me to tame you."

"Stop fooling around and get her in the back seat," Burgess ordered. "Dr. Payne is motioning for us to head out."

Les shoved Mariah into the back with Jake, then fastened her seat belt. And for good measure, he squeezed her left breast. Jake growled. Mariah turned to Jake and gave him a warning glare, sending him a silent message. Please, Jake, don't do anything stupid. Jake quieted and within minutes Burgess started the Saturn and headed out, Agnes and Oliver directly behind them.

In the darkness, Mariah couldn't see anything more than the outline of Jake's face and body, but she could feel him next to her. Feel his heat. Sense his concern. And somehow knowing he was there beside her made the uncertainty more bearable. Neither of them knew what lay ahead. But unless she could come up with an alternate plan, things didn't look good.

They traveled for hours, well into the night. Jake tried to take note of any road signs or markers on their route and he knew Mariah was doing the same. Undoubtedly their captors weren't concerned that Mariah and he might figure out where they were being taken. They had traveled a series of back roads where the traffic was minimal. Guessing at time, Jake figured they had headed up another mountain close to thirty minutes ago. Or was it the same mountain, just on the other side?

Jake prided himself on always being in control of his emotions. Never the type to open a vein and emotionally bleed all over the place. But seeing Agnes and Oliver again had stirred up a hornet's nest of deeply buried anger and hatred. On some level—the primitive level—he wanted to rip out their hearts for what they'd done to his family. But the logical, sensible part of him knew that the best way to exact revenge on the ones who had taken away his family and stolen his father's life-long work was to bring down the Coalition.

When Burgess pulled the Saturn to a stop, Jake glanced outside, but saw nothing but a row of fencing and a large metal gate. The car following them pulled up alongside the SUV and within seconds a gate swung open and the car drove up a winding drive. The SUV followed. Ahead lay a small, isolated cabin. Not new. Not large.

When Agnes and Oliver exited their vehicle, she motioned for Burgess to roll down his window, which he did.

"We'll stay here overnight, then head out first

thing in the morning. I'm lining up a better place to put Jake for safekeeping," Agnes said. "Bring them inside for now."

Jake rubbed his shoulder against Mariah's. He wanted to find a way to reassure her, to remind her that things weren't hopeless. Even if he wasn't so sure himself, he didn't want her to give up hope. Odd how, despite her being such a strong, independent woman, he felt he should be her protector. She might consider herself to be his bodyguard, but in the deepest part of his masculine psyche, he felt that their roles were reversed. Or at least they should be.

Once inside the cold, dank old cabin, Burgess used his flashlight to locate the kerosene lamps that were apparently the only source of light for the place. After the lamps were lit, Agnes ordered Jake and Mariah separated. While he remained in the living room area, Lester took Mariah into what Jake assumed was the kitchen.

Agnes shouted out orders. "Burgess, build a fire in the fireplace and warm this place up. It's freezing in here. And, Oliver, go check on Dr. Brooks. Tell Lester to keep his hands off her."

Jake didn't wait for things to settle down before he repeated his former offer to Agnes. "Let's end this thing here and now. Take me to see Gideon, then set him free and I'll—"

"You are in no position to make a deal," Agnes snapped her reply. "Sit down and shut up."

"My offer won't stand indefinitely," Jake continued, disregarding her warning. "I'll be totally useless to you. Is that what you want? If Gideon is more important to you than I am, then just kill me now and get it over with. Otherwise, I am in a very good position to make a deal."

"Shut the hell up!"

Apparently Agnes didn't deal well with the cold, the dark and Jake's insolence. Keep pushing her, he told himself. Force her to make a decision. Even knowing he couldn't trust her, he was willing to make a deal—he was willing to bargain with the devil if it might give Gideon and Mariah a fighting chance. The only advantage he had was using himself as a bargaining tool. Agreeing to cooperate fully with the Coalition was his only hope of getting Gideon and Mariah out of this damn mess alive. The odds weren't in their favor, but they were the best odds he was going to get.

"What's wrong, Agnes? Are you afraid I'll double-cross you?" Jake goaded her.

She marched over to him, slapped him soundly across the face and replied, "Do you take me for a fool? Of course, you'll double-cross me. As long as we have Gideon, you'll cooperate. If I set him free, you'd stop cooperating."

"Maybe. Maybe not."

"Stop playing games with me, Jake. I'm not releasing Gideon. He's valuable to us in many ways, not only for himself, but as a means of keeping you in line."

Jake grinned. "Then you won't kill Gideon, will you? If you kill him, you lose not only his usefulness to you, but you lose any power you might have over me."

Agnes uttered a feral growl as she realized she and Jake were at a stalemate. No winner. No loser.

"Gag him," Agnes said. "I'm tried of listening to his prattle."

Burgess obeyed instantly, then shoved Jake onto the sofa and gave him an if-you-move-you'll-be-sorry glare. Leaning back into the dilapidated sofa cushions, Jake smiled to himself, then crossed his legs. He might not have won this round, but he was still in the fight.

Agnes turned and headed for the kitchen. As the door swung open, Jake wondered what was happening to Mariah. He had to believe that she could take care of herself since at the present moment there wasn't much he could do to help her.

Lester shoved Mariah into one of the rickety kitchen chairs, then pulled out a chair and draped his legs over the seat as he eased down backward and placed his arms over the back of the chair. Oliver Grimble stood just inside the doorway, apparently keeping an eye on them and waiting for further instructions.

Lester rubbed his hands together. "Why the hell did we come here? This place is a dump. And it's freezing ass cold in here."

"We'll just be here until morning," Oliver replied. "And if I were you, I wouldn't complain in front of my wife. She isn't sympathetic to men who belly-ache."

"A broad with balls of steel, huh?" Lester raked his gaze over Mariah. "I like tough women. You must, too, huh?"

Oliver simply glared menacingly at Lester.

Mariah wondered what was happening in the living room. Was Jake all right? Before she had a chance to really worry, Agnes entered the kitchen. Oliver stood at attention.

"Lester?" Agnes's voice had a sharp edge to it.

"Yes, ma'am?"

"I want you to take our Dr. Brooks for a little ride."

Oliver snapped his head around and stared questioningly at his wife.

"I have no idea whether she's who she represents herself to be or not. And frankly, I don't care. What is obvious is that for whatever reason, she chose Jake Ingram over her loyalty to the Coalition. We don't tolerate that sort of disloyalty. Not for any reason."

"I take it that you don't want Dr. Brooks to come back with me," Lester said.

"That's correct."

"Well, well, looks like old Lester's been given a dirty job, but I promise I'll give you something to smile about before you die." He looked right at Mariah.

"Take her now," Agnes said. "And by all means, do whatever you'd like to her before you dispose of her. Just make sure you dump the body where it won't be found. At least not for a long time. Do you understand?"

"Yes, ma'am." Lester yanked Mariah up out of the chair. "It's party time, Doc."

No. It was decision time, Mariah told herself. If she screamed for help, who would hear her? Jake. And if he tried to help her, he might get hurt. So she was on her own. Better to wait until she was alone with Lester before she made her move. He would try to rape her first, before he killed her. All she had to do was wait for the right moment—then make her move.

"You seem awfully calm for a woman facing death." Agnes studied Mariah closely. "Lester, you'd better watch her. Something tells me that Dr. Brooks has some misguided idea that she can persuade you not to kill her."

"Then she'd be wrong, Dr. Payne. I know how to follow orders."

"You'd better," Agnes told him. "Because if anything goes wrong, you'll pay for your mistake with your life."

Lester gave Mariah a shove toward the door leading into the living room.

"No, wait," Agnes called to him. "Take her out the back door. I'd rather Jake not know anything about this for now. I prefer to tell him in the morning that the good doctor escaped during the night, that she left him behind without another thought.''

Damn the woman! Jake won't believe her, Mariah told herself. He'll know that I'd never willingly desert him. Please, God, please, don't let him lose faith in me.

Within minutes Lester had her out the back door and strapped into the front seat of the Saturn. She wondered if Jake could hear the vehicle's motor roaring to life. What explanation would Agnes and Oliver give him? They'd probably tell him they'd sent Lester off for supplies or some such nonsense.

Lester turned on the radio as he zipped the SUV down the mountainside. A country station blasted out a classic she-done-him-wrong song. Mariah held her breath as he took several dangerous turns at top speed.

''You're in an awful big hurry to kill me, aren't you?'' she asked.

''I'm in a hurry all right,'' he replied. ''But not to kill you. Not for a while. But I am in a hurry to screw you, Doc. And I plan to keep you alive long enough to tire myself out.''

Mariah cringed at the thought. She was at a disadvantage with the handcuffs on, but all she needed was one opportunity—one chance to overpower Lester.

After they'd traveled halfway down the mountain, Lester pulled off on a side road. He drove along until the road forked. She saw the gated gravel road before he did, but the minute he caught a glimpse of it, he got out, then took a pair of wire cutters from the back and locked her inside the SUV. Within minutes he'd cut the chain and latch and swung open the gate, then he got back in the SUV and headed down the private drive. When they came to the end of the driveway, a large building loomed in the darkness. Mariah could make out the silhouette of a massive log cabin.

Lester parked, then unsnapped Mariah's seat belt. "Come on, Doc, get out."

"Where are we?" she asked.

"Looks like some rich guy's home away from home."

"What makes you think no one's here?" Apparently Lester had seen, as she had, the For Sale sign on the gate, the bright-red letters appearing dark-red in the moonlight.

"There was a For Sale sign out front," Lester replied. "Don't pretend you didn't see it."

He reached over and dragged her across the console, then pulled her out of the vehicle. She landed on her feet unsteadily. He grabbed her around the shoulders and forced her into step alongside him. When they reached the front door, he used the butt of his 9 mm to break the stained-glass panel. After sliding his arm through the opening, he unlocked the door from the other side and shoved it open.

All the while Lester pulled her deeper inside the house, Mariah didn't resist. Soon, she told herself. Very soon. He shoved her down on the sofa in the cathedral-ceilinged room, then shrugged off his coat and positioned himself on top of her. His foul breath fanned her face as his tried to kiss her. She turned her head just in time to avoid their lips making contact. Instead he wound up kissing her jaw.

When he started undoing her jacket, she squirmed against him. By the time he had her shirt unbuttoned, she was rubbing herself against his arousal.

"You're getting all excited, aren't you, Doc? You want some really good loving before you die, don't you?"

"You got that right, Les," she said breathlessly— a second before she kneed him in the groin. "I want some good loving—but not from you. Never from you!"

He howled like a wounded coyote. While he was yelping with pain, Mariah managed to knock him off her and onto the floor. Before he had a chance to recover, she used her feet to beat the living daylights out of him. The final blow landed along the side of his face and effectively knocked him senseless. Mariah knelt beside the unconscious Lester, then turned sideways so that she could reach inside his pockets, which was no easy task with her wrists bound together with the metal cuffs. She retrieved what she was fairly certain was the key to the cuffs, but she had a hell of a time inserting the key into the lock. After what seemed like an hour of hit and miss efforts, she finally managed to free herself from the handcuffs.

She raked her hand back into Lester's pants pocket and retrieved the keys to the SUV. But just as she rose to her feet, she heard a noise behind her. When she glanced over her shoulder she saw Lester staring up at her, his 9 mm pointed right at her back.

Eleven

Mariah had looked down the barrel of a gun before, had been faced with danger and even death. Quick and appropriate action had saved her life several times.

"Think you're pretty smart, don't you, Doc?" Lester's hand holding the 9 mm trembled ever so slightly. "Well, you're not. All you did was make me mad and when I'm mad, I'm mean."

Breathe deeply. Stay calm. He's not going to shoot you. Not yet. He wants to make you pay for your actions. Don't do anything hasty. Wait until you're close enough to strike. There was no doubt in Mariah's mind that Lester would give her the opportunity to stop him before he killed her. He was too determined to rape her. He wouldn't kill her yet. Not until he'd satisfied his sick needs.

"Nothing to say?" Lester held out his free hand and motioned to her by crooking his index finger. "Come just a little closer."

She turned around and took several tentative steps toward him.

"That's close enough," he told her. "Now take off your coat."

She removed the coat. If she'd been a few feet closer, she would have tossed it at him, but she was too far away for the tactic to have been effective.

"Now strip, starting with your shirt and bra."

Mariah took her time unbuttoning her shirt, letting Lester's sexual tension build. As she removed her shirt and the frigid air hit her naked arms and shoulders, she shivered. With Lester's gaze glued to her breasts, she was able to move forward a few steps. Instead of removing her bra next, she eased her belt from the loops on the waistband of her slacks.

Realizing she wasn't following his instructions about the order in which he wanted her to disrobe, Lester came toward her, just a few steps, but enough to bring him within range.

"Not the pants next, dammit! Take off your bra. Now!"

Mariah grinned, a seductive, come-hither look in her eyes, and while Lester tried to figure out why she was smiling, she took that final step to put her in a perfect position to act. Before Lester knew what was happening, Mariah brandished her belt, using it like a whip. The thick, supple leather hit Lester's gun hand, snapping loudly as it made contact with his flesh. He yelped in pain and the 9 mm Glock fell from his hand and hit the floor with a resounding thud. Shock registered on Lester's face, then horror, just as Mariah flung herself forward and down, her hands reaching for the weapon lying only a feet inches from Lester's feet.

Her fingers touched the Glock's cold metal surface. Lester bent over and reached for the gun, but Mariah managed to grasp it and pull it to her. He raised his foot, intending to kick Mariah, but she flipped over just in time to avoid his boot connecting with her face. Cursing a blue streak, Lester lunged at her. She rolled over a couple of times. He landed on the floor beside her instead of on top of her as he'd planned. She held the gun in both hands and pointed it directly at his heart.

"Damn bitch!" He growled the words as he rose up and hurled himself at her.

Mariah didn't hesitate, she pulled the trigger—once—and the bullet entered Lester's chest, missing his heart by several inches. As his wiry body came down over her, blood oozing from the wound and dripping onto the floor, she fired a second shot. This one hit the mark. Lester's heart. He dropped like a ten-ton stone. Mariah rolled out of the way as his body crashed to the floor. His blood splattered over her. She jumped to her feet and moved cautiously toward his lifeless body. Using her foot, she rolled him over onto his back. His sightless eyes stared up at the cathedral ceiling. Mariah let out a long, deep breath, relief spreading through her as the rush of adrenaline pumping through her body began to subside.

Ignoring the dead man lying nearby, Mariah picked up her belt, put it on and slid the gun into her hip holster. Not a perfect fit, put close enough. Focusing on what she had to do, she picked up her discarded shirt, then walked over to the sofa, lifted a cotton knit afghan lying across the back and used it to clean Lester's blood off her skin. She hastily put on her shirt before searching the room for a telephone. When she spotted a phone and lifted the receiver, there was no dial tone. Undoubtedly the owners had had the phone disconnected. And her digital phone was back at the cabin in her Chevy Trail-Blazer.

After putting on her coat, she went outside and got in Burgess's Saturn. She wasn't sure she could backtrack to where Agnes and Oliver were holding Jake, but she damn well intended to try. She had two choices—either try to save Jake on her own or risk wasting time by hunting for the nearest town and a telephone. By the time she could get to a town, use a phone and get assistance from fellow agents, it might be too late for Jake. Agnes and Oliver planned to move him to a new location at daybreak. Her best bet was to find her way back to where he was now being held and rescue him before he was moved again. Once there, she could use the micro-transmitter to alert the bureau of the location so they could pick up Agnes and Oliver.

As she started the SUV and turned it around, she wondered if Agnes and Oliver would wonder what was taking Lester so long. Probably not. They had known he intended to rape her before killing her. They probably didn't expect him back for hours. If she was lucky, the gruesome twosome would be asleep and Burgess would have been left to guard Jake. She'd have to park the SUV on the road and walk to the cabin, then break in and get to Jake without alerting the others. And if necessary, she was prepared to kill anyone who got in her way.

Agnes Payne stood over Jake where he was manacled to the ladder-back wooden chair in the corner of the living room. "How does it feel to know that Dr. Brooks has abandoned you, that she chose to save herself and apparently doesn't give a damn what happens to you?"

Jake glared at the manipulative, conniving woman whose ruthless ambition had turned Henry Bloomfield's scientific experiment into a nightmare for his children. When he'd heard a vehicle leaving earlier, he'd questioned Burgess about Mariah, but the man had told him nothing. Then for the past few minutes, Agnes had been trying to torture him with her comments about Mariah's disloyalty. He'd tried to shut out her voice, tried to tell himself that maybe Mariah had escaped, maybe she was safe now. But he knew better. Mariah hadn't abandoned him. She'd been taken away—by Lester.

Jake closed his eyes as Agnes's voice droned on and on, but he could not shut out the pain that gripped him. Mariah alone with Lester. Her hands cuffed and without a weapon. The little monster would rape Mariah first, then kill her. In all his life,

Jake had never known such agony. Every instinct within him wanted to growl like a beast and rip Agnes, Oliver and Burgess apart with his bare hands. Then he wanted to track down Lester and kill him slowly, painfully. The frightening part of this scenario playing inside his head was that he knew he would feel no guilt at killing them, that the primitive, animal side of his nature would actually enjoy it.

Jake had cared for many people. He loved his adoptive parents and his brother, Zach. He'd loved Tara once. And he loved his newfound siblings. And the child in him loved his biological parents. But the love he felt for Mariah surpassed any other love he'd ever known. He didn't understand how it was possible to love someone so fervently, so completely, in such a brief span of time. But he did. The thought of living without Mariah was more than he could bear. Until he'd realized that she was probably dead, he hadn't known the depth of his feelings for her. But now—too late to tell her—he knew.

You can't fall apart, he told himself. It's too late to save Mariah, but you can still save Gideon. And you can bring down the Coalition and make Agnes and Oliver and everyone involved with Code Proteus pay for what they've done—pay dearly.

"He's shut you out, my dear," Oliver Grimble told his wife. "Our Jake seems to have developed the ability to totally control his mind. It will be difficult, if not impossible to ever reprogram him. I see that more plainly now. I should have known that as an adult, he would be the one out of all the children who would be able to resist our control.''

Agnes reached out, grabbed Jake by the chin and forced him to look up at her. "But we can control you, can't we, Jake? As long as we have Gideon, you will do as you're told.''

Jake ignored her completely.

She slapped him on one cheek and then the other. "Respond, damn you!''

He continued ignoring her.

"There are ways to make you suffer. How will you feel watching your brother being tortured?''

The muscles in Jake's jaw tightened, but other than that minuscule reaction, he remained deadly silent, not allowing Agnes the pleasure of a reaction.

"Be that way," she told Jake. "Sooner or later, I'll break you." She turned to Burgess. "Leave him here in this chair all night. Oliver and I will take the bedroom. You can bunk down on the sofa, but keep one eye open until Lester returns from the little errand we sent him to do.''

Agnes eyed Jake. He didn't move a muscle. She huffed loudly, then turned to her husband. "Let's get a few hours sleep. I want to leave here at daybreak.''

Oliver followed his wife into the bedroom, leaving Jake alone with Burgess, who turned and walked over to the sofa. He jerked the one tattered plaid pillow from where it rested in the center of the couch and placed it on the armrest, then lay down. He put his head on the pillow and propped his feet on the opposite sofa arm.

"You behave yourself," Burgess said. "I don't want any trouble out of you."

Jake didn't respond. Just what sort of trouble did the man think he could be with his arms twisted behind the back of the chair, his wrists tightly cuffed and his ankles bound with rope? Apparently Burgess had left the leg irons behind and been forced to make do with rope. But the rope was completely effective. Jake wasn't going anywhere. Not without help. And he had to admit the truth—there was no one to help him. If Mariah was dead—and there was a very good possibility that Lester had killed her—nobody knew where he was. He was completely on his own.

God, Mariah, I hope you didn't suffer. I hope— Emotion lodged in Jake's throat. He wasn't the type of man prone to tears, but at this very moment he longed to cry. Crying might ease the agony trapped deep inside him.

Mariah took more than one wrong turn during her nerve-racking journey of retracing the route Lester had taken last night. But finally, at precisely one-eighteen the next morning, she pulled the Saturn up in front of the gate that led to the small, rustic cabin where she and Jake had been taken the night before, where she prayed Jake was still being held. Before getting out, she searched the SUV thoroughly after parking it on the side of the road. She found ammunition for the Glock—several boxes of clips—and she also found a rifle and another handgun. The weapons might come in handy later. And she'd unearthed a laptop computer, hidden under the front seat. She wasn't sure if it belonged to Burgess or if it was a Coalition issue. She hadn't been issued one, but that didn't necessarily mean anything. Despite her curiosity, examining the computer would have to wait. First things first.

The Bowie knife in a leather sheath that she'd found, she strapped to her calf beneath her slacks. Pulling a knit cap that had probably belonged to Lester down over her head and turning up the collar on her down jacket, she left the Saturn unlocked and headed up the driveway. Snow fell softly, silently, a gentle shower of glistening white shapes moistening her face. The moonlight reflected brightly off the bed of new-fallen snow, lighting the area far more than Mariah would have liked. On a mission such as this, darkness was an ally.

Mariah paused long enough to remove the microtransmitter and send out an SOS. Hopefully she and Jake would be long gone by the time the Feds arrived, but if luck was with her, Agnes, Oliver and Burgess would not escape.

As she approached the cabin, she noted that the only light on inside was the one in the living room, but just a pale glow shown through the dirty window panes. She crept up to the house, then circled it, checking for any sound from inside, but she heard nothing. She peered in each window. The bedroom windows were dark with blinds, but the living room windows were bare and she was able to make out the form of a large man lying on the sofa. Not Jake. The guy was too muscle-bound. As she scanned the room, her heart stopped for a split second when she saw Jake bound to a ladder-back chair. His head was slumped over, but she doubted he was asleep. If she knew Jake, his mind was working at top speed.

Did he think she was dead? What had Agnes and Oliver told him? Whatever lies they'd told him, she knew he hadn't believed them. He must have figured out that they'd sent her away with Lester, that they had intended for Lester to return alone.

Thinking ahead, plotting their escape, Mariah approached Agnes and Oliver's car. Since she couldn't be sure an alarm wouldn't go off if she tampered with the doors, she decided on using a simple method to disable the vehicle. After removing the knife from its sheath, she squatted on her haunches and sliced the passenger side front tire, then she proceeded to inflict similar damage on the other three tires.

Returning to the house, Mariah tried the back door first and to her amazement, it wasn't locked. Were these people so sure they were safe that they hadn't even locked the doors? Of course they thought they were safe. No one—other than she and Lester—had known where they were. And since she was supposed to be dead by now, Burgess had probably left the door unlocked for Lester's return. Well, Lester wouldn't be returning. Not tonight. Not ever again.

But she was back!

Mariah eased open the door. The soft creak sounded loud to her ears, intensified by her nervousness and fear. Yes, she was afraid. She was scared out of her mind. Afraid that she wouldn't be able to rescue Jake.

As she made her way silently out of the kitchen, she passed the closed bedroom door where she supposed Agnes and Oliver lay sleeping. Just as she headed toward the living room, she heard the rumble of voices. She stopped dead in her tracks. With her heart beating wildly and adrenaline rushing through her body, she realized the voices were coming from the bedroom. Agnes and Oliver were not asleep! Damn.

She eased over to the bedroom door and listened.

"I believe we should take Jake directly to the compound in the morning and have Gideon brought there as well," Oliver said. "Until he sees his brother and we make him realize we will sacrifice Gideon, if necessary, Jake isn't likely to cooperate with us."

"I agree with you," Agnes replied. "We should be able to drive to Verde Valley in a few hours. We'll call ahead to the new compound and make sure they're expecting us. I'll tell Willard he can personally sit in on the reunion between Jake and Gideon. He'll enjoy that."

"Yes, he'll enjoy it tremendously."

"We'll have to see that Gideon is moved later tomorrow and brought to Verde Valley so we can facilitate this brotherly reunion very soon. Within the next twenty-four hours. We don't want to rush it. I believe Jake needs some time to stew."

Verde Valley? They were going to bring Gideon Faulkner to a place called Verde Valley. And it was only a few hours drive from here. But where was here? Mariah had no idea where Verde Valley was or if it was an actual location on the map, a real town in Arizona, or if it was simply the name for the Co-alition's new compound. But she had an idea that the bureau knew about this place, even if they didn't know the exact location. The first chance she got, she'd contact her superior and report in. She'd trade information with him. What would she do if Jake didn't want the bureau brought in at this point? Regardless of his reaction, she would have to tell him that she'd already sent out an SOS in the hopes the bureau could nab Agnes and Oliver.

She would just have to figure out all the details later. Right now, she had to get to Jake and set him free without waking Burgess or alerting Agnes and Oliver. Easy as pie, her inner voice told her sarcastically.

Years of training had taught her how to maneuver silently under the worst circumstances, but to be prepared for the unknown in every situation. She approached the living room, studied the area and its contents, as well as Burgess, snoring where he lay on the sofa, and Jake, head bent and quiet, in the straight-back chair. Quickly, deftly, barely breathing, she went directly to Jake, whose head snapped up when she reached him. Their gazes met and locked in the semidarkness. She recognized the relief in his eyes. And something more. Happiness? Love? His mouth opened, but when she shook her head, he nodded, indicating that he understood the need for absolute silence. She worked hurriedly to untie the rope binding his legs and as the knots loosened, she lowered the rope to the floor. Jake lifted his feet up and over the rope. Then Mariah slipped her hand into her pocket and pulled out the keys that had freed her from her cuffs, hoping they would also fit Jake's. She inserted the key in the lock and—presto—the metal restraints opened. With the utmost ease, Jake removed the cuffs and when he stood, he laid them quietly in the seat of the chair.

Burgess snorted. Mariah froze to the spot. Jake stood rigid and unmoving. Burgess sucked in air and began snoring monotonously again. Mariah led Jake toward the kitchen.

She grasped the knob and cracked open the door. It squeaked softly as it had when she'd entered the cabin.

"That you, Lester?" Burgess called out, his voice heavy with sleep.

Damn! Mariah flung open the door. She and Jake broke into a full run, straight down the road. The frigid predawn air cut through her clothing like razor-sharp blades. By the time they were halfway to the main road where the Saturn was parked, her chest ached. From somewhere behind them she heard shouting, voices echoing in the mountain stillness. Burgess had no doubt awakened fully and alerted Agnes and Oliver. But if they followed Jake and her, they'd have to do so on foot. With four slashed tires, their car wasn't going anywhere.

The open gate lay ahead, only a few yards away. Jake kept pace with her. He didn't seem to even be breathing hard. When they reached the Saturn, she jumped behind the wheel as Jake slid into the passenger seat. Just as she inserted the key and started the SUV, a rifle shot rang out, followed by another. The second shot hit the right rear door.

Mariah revved the engine, shoved the gears into drive and raced off, leaving behind a cloud of fresh snow and loose gravel.

Twelve

"Just what the hell happened?" Agnes Payne yelled at the top of her lungs as she glared menacingly at Burgess.

Oliver had seen his wife in a fit of rage on numerous occasions and he usually did his best to steer clear of her. But there was no escape. He sincerely hoped she didn't kill Burgess on the spot. He'd known her to shoot first and ask questions later.

"Hell, if I know." Burgess's deep voice quivered. "I swear I thought I heard Lester coming in and then I realized Ingram was gone and—"

Agnes slapped Burgess soundly. The big man looked at her, slightly dazed, fear in his eyes. "You fool. Do you know what your negligence has cost us? Jake Ingram was the prize—the grand prize. And you've allowed him to escape."

"But how was I to know that Dr. Brooks would get away from Lester? She should be dead, shouldn't she?"

"Yes, she most definitely should be dead," Agnes replied, her tone minacious and condescending. "But my guess is that Lester is the one who's dead. And you know what that means?"

Burgess shook his head.

Perhaps Burgess didn't know what Dr. Brooks's escape from Lester meant, but Oliver suspected he knew. Dr. Brooks was not a psychiatrist, not a loyal Coalition member who'd been swayed by Jake Ingram's charm. She was probably a government agent of some sort. Highly trained. Not only smarter than Lester and Ingram, but possessing the ability to overpower a man twice her size.

"It means that our Dr. Brooks is probably a federal agent," Agnes said. "Someone trained in self-defense."

"If you thought she might be an agent, why did you think Lester could handle her?" Burgess asked. "Isn't it partly your fault?"

No, no, Oliver wanted to say, but kept quiet. Burgess had done the wrong thing by trying to shift any part of the blame onto Agnes. As Oliver suspected she would do, she slapped Burgess again. The man glowered at her; his hand tightened around the rifle he held.

"We're wasting valuable time, my dear." Oliver dared to voice an opinion. "We should contact headquarters and have someone come for us as soon as possible."

The sound of Oliver's voice—the voice of calm and reason—seemed to soothe her for the moment. She nodded, then said, "Yes, of course. I'll make the call. We can deal with Burgess later."

The minute Agnes went inside the cabin to contact

their new headquarters here in Arizona, Burgess turned to Oliver. "It wasn't my fault. You know it wasn't."

"If you'd been alert, it wouldn't have happened. Therefore, it is your fault."

"But you heard her say that—"

"Never contradict my wife. Your best defense is to admit guilt and beg her forgiveness."

Burgess shifted his feet restlessly, as if he needed to go to the bathroom. It became apparent that the man was more than just nervous because of Agnes's tongue-lashing.

"Is there something else?" Oliver asked. "Some problem we don't know about?"

"What—what else could there be?"

"You tell me."

Burgess shrugged.

"If you're hiding something, you'd better tell me now. If Agnes finds out about whatever it is, you'll need me on your side if you don't want her to kill you."

"She'd actually kill me? God, man, I'd heard rumors about her, but—"

"Never listen to rumors," Oliver told him. "Listen to a man who's been at her side for over thirty years. You do not screw around with Agnes Payne."

"Look, it was Lester's idea to take the damn thing when we picked up Ingram at Redcom."

"What thing did you pick up?"

"The laptop. I knew I shouldn't have listened to

that idiot, but he said we could sell it and make a few extra bucks.''

"A laptop computer? You stole a computer from Redcom?''

"It was in the room with Ingram when we picked him up for transport. It was just sitting there on the desk and Lester grabbed it while I hoisted Ingram over my shoulder.''

The blood ran cold in Oliver's veins. He suspected that Lester had stolen one of the laptops used throughout the complex in Oregon—a direct link to the Coalition's main computer system.

"Where is that computer now?'' Oliver asked. "Is it back at the cabin where you first took Ingram?''

Burgess shook his head.

"Then where is it?''

"It's in the Saturn. Under the front seat.''

"Damn!'' Oliver grabbed Burgess by the coat lapels and shook him, disregarding the fact that the man was half a foot taller and outweighed him by more than fifty pounds.

"Dr. Brooks might not find it,'' Burgess said as he freed himself from Oliver's tenacious hold. "Why would she look under the front seat?''

"Because, you fool, if she is a trained agent, as we suspect, she'll go over that SUV with a fine-tooth comb.'' Oliver turned and headed toward the house.

"Do you have to tell Dr. Payne?''

"Of course I have to tell her. If that laptop is what I suspect it is, it is most likely linked directly to our computer at both the Oregon compound and the new compound at Verde Valley.''

"Holy sh— I screwed up big time, huh?''

''Yes, Mr. Burgess, you most certainly screwed up big time.''

About a mile down the road, Jake caught his breath enough to actually talk. Everything had happened so fast that he hadn't had time to think, only to act and react. He'd been so sure Mariah was dead, certain that Lester had raped and then killed her. But he should have known that if any woman could escape, Mariah could. Remember, she's a highly trained federal agent, he told himself. And you've witnessed, firsthand, what an expert she is at martial arts. She probably outsmarted Lester and took the first opportunity to overpower the bastard. Jake hoped like hell that the man was dead.

''Want to tell me what happened?'' Jake stared at Mariah, her dark silhouette clearly visible within the SUV.

''Lester's orders were to kill me. Naturally, he tried to rape me first. I decided he wasn't going to do either. I got the upper hand and shot him. Twice. He's dead.''

''And instead of going for help, you decided to come to my rescue on your own, huh?''

''Something like that. I knew Agnes and Oliver were planning on moving you first thing in the morning. I couldn't risk waiting. If they'd moved you, we might not have been able to track you.''

''Stop for a few minutes, will you?''

Mariah hazarded a glance at Jake while driving at top speed down the icy mountain road. ''What?''

''Stop the truck. Just for two minutes.''

Mariah slowed the SUV, then stopped right in the middle of the desolate road, shifting into idle and leaving the motor running. When she turned to him, expecting him to say something, she got quite a surprise. Jake reached across the console and grabbed her face with his open palms, then brought his mouth down on hers and kissed her. He kept kissing her until they were both breathless. Then he lifted his head, caressed her cheek and smiled.

''Lady, I thought you were dead. Do you have any idea how that made me feel?''

''Sad?''

''Devastated.''

''Really?'' Tears glistened in her eyes.

''Mariah Daley, when this crazy business is all over—''

She put two fingers to his lips. ''I thought we weren't going to make any promises.''

''No promises. Not yet. Hell, we don't know if either one of us will come out of this mess alive. But you need to know...I need to tell you... When I thought Lester had killed you, I realized exactly how much you mean to me. More than anything or anyone. More than my own life.''

"Oh, Jake. Dammit."

Using his fingertip, he wiped away the lone tear that escaped from her eye. "Now, let's get moving again. We can talk while you drive."

"Hey, who's the federal agent around here anyway? I'm the one who's supposed to be in charge."

"With us, it'll always be a toss-up as to who's the boss. Maybe we should just agree right now to take turns."

Mariah shifted gears and put her foot on the gas. "Today is my turn," she told him.

"Any particular reason you want to be the boss today?"

"Because I want to call my superior at the bureau and—"

"No way! If I hadn't been so damn relieved to see you alive, I'd have questioned you before we hightailed it out of there. Just how do you propose we find Gideon now that we've escaped?"

"You left with me because you knew that if Agnes and Oliver caught me, they would kill me. You put my safety above everything else. Don't you think I know—"

"You come first, Mariah," he told her. "Is that what you wanted to hear? But that doesn't mean I've given up on finding Gideon or on recovering the computer disk."

"I didn't think that's what it meant. However, we're going to need the bureau to help us. I know where the new compound is and I overheard Agnes and Oliver discussing bringing Gideon there to set up a reunion between you two brothers.''

''When did you hear this? Where's the compound?''

''I overheard them talking right before I freed you. The Arizona compound is somewhere near a place called Verde Valley.''

''Is that a town?'' Jake asked.

''I have no idea. That's why I have to get in touch with Johnson, my immediate superior. He can help us. I have a feeling they already know about this place and if they don't, then they have the equipment and manpower to locate it before we can. Unless…''

''Unless what?''

''Unless a certain laptop computer stashed away under my seat might be able to give us the information we need.''

''And just where did this laptop come from?'' Jake asked.

''I'm not certain, but when I searched the Saturn before I came in to rescue you, I found it under the seat. My guess is that it belongs to Burgess or Lester. And since neither seem the type to own a laptop—''

''They stole it.'' Jake slapped his hand down on his thigh.

''And if—and that's a big if—they stole it from the Coalition, then maybe, just maybe, it will be useful to us.''

''Stop the truck again,'' Jake demanded.

"What?"

"Stop, give me the laptop and I'll take a look at it while you drive."

"Other than as fast and far away from Dr. Payne and her hubby, where do you suggest we go? We have no idea where Verde Valley is."

"We'll drive to the nearest town, ditch this SUV and find us another vehicle."

"I suggest we check into a motel, get a few hours rest and a hot shower, then grab a bite to eat—after I contact Johnson."

"We won't make any definite decisions until after I take a look at the laptop. Agreed?"

Mariah stopped the SUV again, long enough for Jake to pull the laptop out from underneath her seat. He placed the computer case in his lap, unzipped it and looked inside. "Well, look at this. There's a hookup for the charger that connects to the cigarette lighter. How convenient."

"Maybe too convenient. What if the thing is booby-trapped? What if when you turn it on, it explodes? Or what if it triggers a bomb planted somewhere in the truck?"

"Damn, I like the way your mind works. Being a fed has taught you to be suspicious, to take nothing at face value. But you know this laptop looks just like the one I saw where I was held at the Oregon compound."

"Hmm, interesting. So, do you turn it on or not?" Mariah asked.

"I say we risk it. What do you think? Your decision. After all, you wanted to be the boss for today."

"All right. If I'm the boss, then give me the laptop and we'll both get out of the truck. We'll get far enough away from the vehicle to be relatively safe. You go in one direction and I'll go in the other, then I'll turn on the computer and we'll see what happens."

"Sounds like a reasonable plan," Jake said. "Except for one thing."

"What?"

Before Mariah realized his intentions, Jake flung open the passenger door and jumped down onto the pavement. He looked back at her and said, "I'll turn on the computer. You run in the opposite direction."

"Dammit, Jake, I'm the boss today. I'm the federal agent. I'm the bodyguard."

"Yeah, honey, I know." He started walking away, then called back to her. "But I'm the man, and to me that means I'm your protector, not the other way around."

Without protest—apparently because she knew protesting would be useless—Mariah jumped out of the SUV and ran in the opposite direction. When he reached a distance he deemed somewhat safe, Jake squatted on his haunches, set the laptop carrying case down, then lifted the lid slowly, cautiously. He took a deep breath and uttered a quick prayer before activating the computer.

* * *

Mariah prayed, begging the Good Lord to help them. Don't let anything happen to Jake. If I lose him, I'll have no reason to live. She stopped running when she felt she had reached a safe distance, then she turned around and looked toward Jake.

"It's on," he shouted. "No bomb. No explosions."

"Not yet."

"Are you expecting a delayed reaction?"

"Maybe."

"Okay, we'll wait. Is five minutes long enough?" he asked. "I sure hope so. It's damn cold out here."

"You're worried about being cold?" Much too far away from him to have any idea what he was typing, she watched while Jake tapped on the keyboard.

"From what I can tell, this isn't a weapon of any kind. And the battery needs recharging. But I know one thing for sure—I need the modem connected to a telephone as soon as possible."

Mariah walked in place, trying to stay warm. The effort proved useless. It took her all of three minutes to shout at Jake, "Let's get back in the truck and find a town. We'll abandon the truck and either hide it somewhere or camouflage it in some way. It's only a matter of time before Agnes and Oliver have their Coalition goons canvassing everywhere within a hundred-mile range of where we left them."

Jake met her on her side of the SUV. "Why don't you rest for a while and let me drive?"

"Because you're the man and—"

He shoved the laptop at her and said, "Because you've had a rough time and you could use a little rest. Okay?"

"Okay."

As she took the laptop and rounded the Saturn's hood, she wondered why it was that allowing Jake to treat her like a woman, all possessive and protective and caring, didn't bring her I-am-woman-hear-me-roar instincts into full force. Perhaps it's because Jake doesn't make you feel as if you can't take care of yourself. He just makes you feel like taking care of you is the most important thing in the world to him.

Mariah got in on the passenger side, placed the laptop on the floorboard, then connected her safety belt. "Buckle up," she told Jake, humor in her voice. "We've been breaking the law traveling without our seat belts hooked up."

Jake buckled up, then started the truck. He glanced at the dashboard. "Do you realize we're nearly out of gas?"

"Oh, great. No, I didn't realize it. But then checking the gas gauge was the last thing on my mind."

"How close to empty are we?"

"Damn close," he told her. "My guess is we might have twenty, possibly twenty-five miles worth of gas left."

"Then let's hope we find a service station sometime soon."

"If we don't, we'll be abandoning the SUV a lot sooner than we'd planned."

Shortly after Agnes Payne telephoned for help, a Coalition helicopter arrived to pick them up. And Oliver wasn't the least bit surprised when she gave Burgess bad news.

"You're to stay here," Agnes told the man. "Someone will come by in a few hours and pick you up. I suggest your prepare yourself to be severely punished, Mr. Burgess."

When he boarded the chopper, Oliver gave Burgess a sympathetic glance.

"I expect whatever branch of the government Dr. Brooks is working for will have agents here within another hour," Agnes said.

"And you've left Burgess there? He'll talk. He'll tell them—"

"Burgess is an underling. He knows nothing important about Coalition business."

"He can identify you and me."

Oliver glanced out at Burgess standing in the driveway at the cabin, clearly visible in the moonlight brightly reflected off the snow. Suddenly the man froze, a stricken look on his face. He dropped to the ground. Dead. Oliver gasped, then jerked around and looked behind him. A Coalition soldier pulled in his rifle—the rifle that had effectively silenced Burgess. Permanently. Oliver realized that he should have known Agnes would leave behind no witnesses.

"When will you ever learn, Oliver dear, that I always think of everything."

Not everything, Oliver thought. You haven't even guessed that Burgess and Lester stole a laptop computer from the Oregon compound and at this very minute Dr. Brooks and Jake Ingram are in possession of that valuable item.

"Agnes, I must tell you something."

"What is it, Oliver?"

"Well, it seems that when Burgess and Lester picked up Jake at Redcom, they—er, actually Lester stole something from the room where Jake was being held."

He felt his wife's body tensing, sensed her barely suppressed anger. "What did that fool Lester steal?"

"A laptop."

Agnes's face flushed scarlet. No doubt, her blood pressure rose by several degrees. "And where is that laptop now?"

"Under the driver's seat of the Saturn Burgess was driving."

"The SUV Lester took when we sent Dr. Brooks with him?"

"Yes, that very same SUV."

"And Jake and Dr. Brooks escaped in that vehicle."

"Yes, they did."

"Then it's a good thing Burgess is dead and Lester, too, probably. Otherwise, I'd kill both of them myself. If it's a Redcom laptop, there's a good chance it is linked directly to the Coalition's main computers. You do realize what it means if Jake and Mariah find that laptop, don't you?''

"Yes, my dear, I have a pretty good idea.''

Agnes grabbed the helicopter pilot's arm. "Take off immediately. And contact headquarters as soon as possible. We have a major problem on our hands.''

The small whirlybird lifted off, blowing loose snow in every direction. All the while Agnes ranted, and Oliver and the other two men aboard had no choice but to endure her tirade.

Thirteen

Fortunately, Jake and Mariah came upon a town before running out of gas. After ditching the SUV, hiding it behind an abandoned gas station on the outskirts of Eagle Springs, they trekked into town, an unincorporated wide-place-in-the-road. Since it wasn't quite four in the morning, the place was dead. No sign of life anywhere, only the eerie glow of half a dozen streetlights. The snow had tapered off to a few stray flakes ten miles back and had now stopped completely, leaving about two fresh inches of the white stuff. By the time they reached the center of Main Street, Mariah was beginning to think they'd have to backtrack to the SUV and hit the road again. But suddenly she noticed a flickering neon light ahead.

"Is that what I think it is?"

"I believe we've found a motel," Jake said.

"I'm surprised this place has one."

They picked up their pace, all but running as they headed down the only street lined with businesses and went straight out of town in the opposite direction. When they came to the building beneath the neon sign flashing Eagle Springs Motel, they paused long enough to inspect the place. The one-level motel, probably originally built in the fifties, was constructed of cinder blocks painted a vivid turquoise. Mariah counted ten units—ten doors, each with bright red numbers painted in the center.

"I never thought the prospect of sharing quarters with cockroaches would actually be appealing," Mariah said.

Jake chuckled. "It doesn't look like much, I admit, but it might be a lot cleaner than you think."

"At this point, I just want to get in out of the freezing cold so we can inspect the laptop and make some informed decisions."

"Then let's see if there's a room available." Jake scanned the parking area. There were only two vehicles. "On second thought, I doubt that will be a problem."

Mariah followed behind him as he went directly to the door marked Office. He opened the door and they went inside, the warmth of the interior hitting them the minute they entered. Sitting behind the counter, a fat, bald man snored loudly. Jake marched up to what passed as a front desk and slammed his hand down repeatedly on the metal ringer. The man's eyelids popped open and he all but fell out of his chair.

"Yes, sir. What can I do for you and the Mrs.?" The man rubbed his hand over his mouth as he stood up.

"We'd like a room," Jake said.

"It's fifty-nine a night and if you're planning on staying past our eleven-o'clock checkout, it'll be another fifty-nine."

Jake's eyes widened as he glanced at Mariah, apparently only now realizing that neither of them had any money. Mariah smiled, reached inside her coat pocket and pulled out a billfold, then removed a credit card and held it out to the desk clerk. Before the man could take the card, Jake grabbed her arm and pulled her aside.

"You've got a credit card?"

"Yes, I do. No one bothered to check my clothes for a wallet. I have two credit cards, a driver's license and forty dollars in cash. All the ID is fake, of course," Mariah whispered. "It's all under the name Dr. Mariah Brooks."

"And if we use the credit card—"

"It won't matter. By the time anyone tries to trace it, this whole thing will be history."

"Right." Jake took the credit card from her and handed it to the desk clerk. "Sorry about that. I felt I should put the room on my card, but my wife insists on putting it on hers."

"Whatever." The desk clerk shrugged. "How many nights?"

"Two," Mariah replied, asking for two nights just in case they were here past the eleven o'clock checkout time today.

The man yawned, took the credit card, ran it through the machine, then handed Mariah an ink pen and the bill to sign. After she scribbled her alias, he gave her a key. "Room Six."

As they made their way down the cracked concrete walkway, Jake's arm around Mariah's shoulders, she said, "He didn't look at the credit card or ask for other ID or inquire about our luggage. And he didn't even notice we showed up without a car."

"Yeah, lucky for us he wasn't very observant, huh?"

Giving him a sidelong glimpse, she noticed his big smile. "Ha-ha. I'm glad you've been able to keep your sense of humor."

Jake unlocked the door to Room Six and flipped on a light to reveal a surprisingly clean, neat room. The walls were painted a dark gold, the brickred curtains contrasting nicely and matching the quilted bedspread. The bed, nightstand and dresser were all a cheap wood veneer, punctured here and there with nicks and scratches. Mariah instantly went into federal-agent mode and inspected the room thoroughly, pointing out the phone to Jake before going into the bathroom.

"There's a coffee machine, so if you'd like coffee, I'll put some on in a few minutes," she told him, then turned on the sink faucets. "And there's hot water." She glanced around the room. "Four white towels and washcloths." She whipped back the shower curtain, then flipped up the commode lid. "You were right. This place is a lot cleaner than I expected."

After taking the time to wash away the faint stains from Lester's dried blood that had splattered on her, Mariah returned to the bedroom. Jake already had the computer modem connected to the telephone, the laptop plugged in to the electrical outlet and he was typing something on the keyboard.

Planting her hands on her hips, she said, "You didn't waste any time, did you?"

She knew exactly what she should do—call Johnson and let the FBI take things from here. But she couldn't do that. Not unless Jake agreed. And what were the odds that he'd trust anyone other than himself to rescue Gideon? Dammit, didn't he realize that despite his superhero qualities, he was not really a superhero? He was just a guy with a genius IQ and a perfect body.

"Jake?"

"Huh?" He didn't glance up from the computer.

"We need to talk."

"We will. Later."

She sat down on the edge of the bed beside him, reached over and pressed the lid down on the laptop. He jerked his hands back and looked at her.

"Sorry," he said. "You wanted to talk and I wasn't paying attention to you."

"Jake, whatever is on this computer, even if it helps us discover God knows what about the Coalition, we've reached a point where we can't do this alone. I know you want to save your brother, but we need help."

"You're right. We do."

Had she heard him correctly? Had Jake actually agreed that they needed help? "I want to call Johnson and tell him—"

"Is Johnson in Arizona?"

"Yes, he is. Why?"

"And can he get a helicopter to land him just about anywhere?"

"Yes, of course, but—"

"Call him around eight o'clock," Jake said. "But don't tell him anything except to meet you at ten o'clock at the abandoned gas station where we left the truck."

"I don't understand."

"At ten o'clock, the Coalition will know I have this computer and they'll know my location. They'll send someone for me. Maybe Agnes will come herself."

"Jake, you aren't making any sense." Mariah didn't like this. She didn't like it one little bit. Jake had devised some sort of plan without even discussing it with her. A plan that separated them. A plan that put him right back in Coalition hands. "Whatever you're planning, forget it if it involves your turning yourself back over to Agnes and Oliver."

Jake shoved the laptop off his thighs and onto the bed, then he grabbed Mariah by the shoulders. "I'm ninety-nine percent sure that this laptop is linked to the Coalition's main computer, but there are all sorts of password safeguards. It's something Gretchen could probably handle in an hour or two, but I can't get into it that fast and neither can you. So when you leave, you take the laptop with you and see that it gets in the right hands and straight to my sister.''

''And while I'm meeting Johnson and giving him the laptop, what will you be doing?''

''I'll be right here waiting for the Coalition to come after me. By then they'll be aware that I've tried to hack into their main computer and inadvertently gave away my location.''

Mariah grabbed his arm. ''What you're thinking of doing is too risky. If you allow them to recapture you—''

''I have to take that risk if we're going to rescue Gideon, get our hands on that computer disk and bring down the Coalition once and for all. I want to make sure Code Proteus is abandoned, that no more genetically engineered children will become lab experiments and be used by power-hungry people.'' Jake took her hand into his. ''Explain my plan to Johnson. Tell him it's my way or not at all. If he agrees to allow me to be recaptured, then you can tail us to Verde Valley. Once I'm sure Gideon is safe, I'll signal you.''

''How do you intend to—'' She noticed Jake glance at her boots. ''You want my microtransmitter. But where will you hide it?''

''It's small enough to slip down into my sock and inside my shoe. I doubt they'll strip me. Frisk me, maybe, but not make me take off my socks and boots.''

"Do you know how many things could go wrong? And I won't be there with you. You'll be on your own until—'' Mariah swallowed hard. "If anyone else had come up with this plan...if you weren't involved, I'd say it's a damn good plan. But I don't happen to be in love with anyone else.''

Jake ran his fingers up Mariah's back in a slow, seductive caress, then slipped his hand beneath her hair and grasped the back of her neck. "We've got a few hours before we put my plan into motion. I don't think we should waste our time together.''

No, they shouldn't waste these few precious hours. He didn't say it, but she knew he was thinking exactly what she was—that these could be the last hours they would ever spend together. There was no guarantee that Jake would come back to her. Without their voicing her fears, she understood that he was still willing to sacrifice his life to save his brother and to bring down the Coalition. In her book, that made Jake Ingram a true superhero.

Mariah pulled Lester's Glock out of her hip holster and laid it on the floor, then she threw herself at Jake. Her mouth claimed his, kissing him, tasting him, wanting never to forget anything about him. How he looked, how his voice sounded, the way he tasted, his unique scent, the feel of him, his body against hers, his lips on hers. There would never be anyone else for her. Only Jake. Now and forever.

Her hands worked feverishly to yank off his coat. Once that was accomplished, she went to work on his shirt, becoming frustrated when the buttons wouldn't undo fast enough to suit her. She stripped him to the waist, then toppled him over onto the bed, all the while kissing him. Easing her mouth away from his, she licked a path from his chin to his belt buckle. When she undid the buckle, he grabbed her and flipped her onto her back, then tore at her clothes, divesting her of her coat first. She helped him get rid of her shirt and bra in record time. He pulled her into his arms. Her breasts crushed against his chest. Every nerve tingled. Her femininity clenched and unclenched in preparation. Moisture collected between her thighs.

They rolled and tumbled on the bed, wrinkling the spread, knocking pillows aside, as they removed the rest of their clothes and devoured each new inch of exposed flesh. While she undid her boots, Jake sat behind her, her buttocks firmly pressed against his sex. Her nipples peaked as he lifted her breasts from behind and his thumbs skillfully stroked each tip until they were pebble hard. She kicked off her boots, which dropped to the floor, then she shucked off her socks.

"You did such a good job with yours, why don't you take off mine, too," he told her.

Jake's lips moved up and down her neck, spreading quick, hot kisses. Then his tongue replaced his lips and just as she removed his left boot, his teeth nipped her neck. Mariah cried out when the pleasure/ pain ripped through her. With her body angled slightly forward so she could reach his other foot, Jake leaned his head just enough so that he could lick her back, from the nape to the hollow at the base of her spine. She whimpered and squirmed. And the minute she finished getting rid of his socks and other shoe, she turned on him and flung her arms around his neck, effectively knocking him flat on his back again.

He gazed up at her and grinned. "I forgot that you're the boss today."

"Damn straight, I'm the boss." She wanted him so much she didn't think she could bear to wait another minute. She ached with the need to have him inside her, to take him and take him until she was spent. And then do it all over again. These next few hours could be a lifetime. Their lifetime together.

She straddled his hips, lifted herself up and over his erection, then impaled herself on his sex. A cry of sheer feminine satisfaction erupted from deep inside her. Being with him this way felt so good. He felt so good.

"I take it that you're not a lady who needs a lot of foreplay," Jake said teasingly.

"Not when the man is you," she told him. "And not when I'm hurting for you so bad I can't stand it."

He bucked his hips, thrusting up and deep inside her. She threw back her shoulders and tossed back her head just before she set the pace. Jake caressed her hips and stroked his fingertips over her buttocks. Lifting her. Maneuvering her. She rode him like a madwoman, increasing the speed to a breakneck, pulsating rhythm. Her climax built quickly—too quickly. She didn't want it to end so fast, but she could do little to stop the avalanche of release once it began. Crying out with pure pleasure when fulfillment claimed her, Mariah collapsed on top of Jake and let the aftershocks radiate through her body. And while those sweet tremors rippled along her oversensitive nerve endings, Jake reversed their positions and came down on top of her, sweat glistening on his muscular chest. He thrust deep and hard. Once. Twice. And then he came apart after the third lunge, his own climax shattering him into a million pieces.

Afterward they lay there in each other's arms, their breathing gradually slowing, and kissed each other between murmured words. Mariah closed her eyes as she snuggled close to Jake and wondered if any moment in her life after this one would ever be as perfect. She lost track of the time, had no idea how long they lay there together, sated, happy, momentarily content. Jake roused first, sitting up and moving to the edge of the rumpled bed. He stood and held out his hand to her.

"How about a shower?" he asked, a wickedly lascivious grin on his face.

"You scrub my back, I'll scrub yours." She jumped out of bed, grabbed his hand and frolicked across the room with him, but her gaze caught a glimpse of morning sunlight peeping through the cheap plastic blinds at the lone window in the room. Ignore the time, she told herself. Pretend this is only the first morning of many you and Jake will spend together.

Jake turned on the shower and they waited until the water warmed before stepping beneath the peppering spray. Her eyes devoured Jake. Every inch of his large, sleek body was sheer perfection. Reaching out, she ran her hands over his chest, down across his navel and then forked her fingers through the jet black hair surrounding his impressive sex.

He grabbed her hand to stop her from touching him. She looked quizzically at him.

"I want foreplay this time," he told her. "That means you behave yourself until I've done everything to you I want to do."

"Ooh, that sounds like a threat."

"It is. I'm threatening to drive you wild with desire until you're begging me to make love to you."

"I thought we'd already done that," she said. "Me wild with desire and begging you to—"

"I didn't hear any begging. I heard orders from the boss lady."

Mariah laughed. "Well, if you want me to beg, you're going to have to—"

He dove down and sucked the nipple on her right breast into his mouth while his other hand slipped between her feminine folds and rubbed her intimately. She gasped, the pleasure instant and intense. Moaning softly, she gave herself over to him completely, allowing him to do with her as he willed.

"Jake?"

"Hmm?" He released her nipple for a second.

"What else…ah…do you…oh, yes…have in mind doing to me?"

While the warm water cascaded over their hot, naked bodies, Jake planted a series of kisses from her breasts to her belly, then eased down on his knees and spread her legs apart. He told her, in earthy, graphic words and phrases exactly what he was going to do to her. Mariah braced herself by placing her hands on his shoulders while his mouth and tongue went into action. As he stroked her into a frenzy, he clutched her buttocks, pressing her against his face. At the very instant she gasped with release, Jake rose up, pushed her against the wall and lifted her enough so that he could fit himself inside her. And while her climax tapered off into aftershocks, he held her hips and pumped into her again and again and again.

"I like your idea of foreplay," she said breathlessly, then draped her legs around him and held on for dear life as he pounded deeper and faster. And harder.

Mariah's mind was so fuzzy from passion and pleasure that she didn't even think how remarkable it was that she was on the brink of a second orgasm—not until she climaxed simultaneously with Jake. A few minutes later, he slid her down his body, reached outside the shower and yanked a washcloth off the rack, then lathered it with soap and began washing Mariah's back. She closed her eyes and savored the experience. When he finished, she took the washcloth and familiarized herself with his body as intimately as he had hers.

Mariah had telephoned Johnson from a pay phone in the ladies' room of the only cafe in town and told him when and where to meet her. He'd tried to question her further, but she'd hung up on him. She'd taken breakfast back to the motel for Jake and her, but neither of them had had much appetite, then at nine-fifteen, she'd kissed him goodbye and walked away. She had wanted to look back at him, but she hadn't.

She had now been waiting inside the abandoned gas station just outside Eagle Springs for at least ten minutes. Don't think about what will happen if Johnson doesn't agree to Jake's plan, she told herself. If Johnson says no, then you'll have to knock him out and go it alone. No way in hell was she going to let Jake be recaptured by the Coalition without her being right behind him, tracking him every mile of the way to Verde Valley, wherever the hell that was. When she inquired about Verde Valley at the cafe, no one had ever heard of the place.

At one minute after ten, a dark, nondescript sedan pulled up outside the gas station. Mariah glanced through the station's dirty, cracked windowpanes and immediately recognized her boss as he emerged from the car. He was alone, just as she'd requested. Of course, that didn't mean he didn't have backup half a mile down the road.

She waited for him to come to her. He studied the deserted building, then walked all the way around it before trying the door. The rusty hinges creaked as he eased the door open. He drew his Smith & Wesson before he entered.

"Daley?" he called her name.

Mariah came out of the shadows and showed herself.

"Where's Jake Ingram?" he asked.

"That's what we have to talk about."

"Your assignment was to bring Ingram to us so that we can keep him safe."

"I know what my assignment was, but things have changed."

Johnson lifted a skeptical eyebrow. "I haven't been informed of any change."

"That's what I'm going to do—inform you of a change in plans."

At twenty-eight minutes past eleven, Mariah and Johnson watched while Agnes Payne and Oliver Grimble, aided by four suited men, walked Jake out of Room Six at the Eagle Springs Motel and straight to a waiting gray van. Jake didn't put up a fuss and to any unsuspecting soul looking on, it appeared that he went with his captors willingly. And in a way, that was exactly what he'd done, Mariah thought. Her noble superhero. A man who would sacrifice his own life to save his brother and destroy an evil empire.

Although realistically she knew she had to stay put, had to wait and could do nothing but follow at a very discreet distance, every feminine instinct in her wanted to run to Jake, her "borrowed" Glock blazing bullets as she rushed in to save him, not only from the Coalition, but from his own nobility. As soon as the van disappeared down the road leading back toward downtown Eagle Springs, Mariah and Johnson jumped in his sedan and headed out after them.

Not for one second during their journey would they be within sight of the van taking Jake to Verde Valley and possibly to his death. With only a minimum of time to coordinate the operation, her boss had lined up a squad of federal and state agents who would take part in tracking the van from Eagle Springs to its destination. Keeping in contact via digital phones with scrambled frequencies, a series of cars would follow the van, each for no more than two miles, and would always keep a discreet distance between their vehicle and the van.

Once Jake was inside the Arizona compound, the federal agents would move in and position themselves, waiting for Jake's signal. On his command, they would storm the complex, blasting their way inside if necessary. Johnson had agreed that Mariah

could be in the forefront of the invasion, although to
be honest with herself, she knew his permission
hadn't been essential. With Jake's life on the line,
she intended to lead the advance attack and nobody
had damn well better try to stop her.

Fourteen

The new Arizona Coalition compound where Agnes and Oliver took Jake was underground, in what Jake figured had once been gold mine country. The rocky roadbed, with signs of long-ago mining camps, came to an end on the snow-covered mountainside. There was no paved road, no high gates connected to winding chain-link fencing. Nothing to make the place resemble a government installation or a private facility. Although there were no armed guards to be seen anywhere, he suspected the place was as secure as Fort Knox. The driver stopped directly in front of what appeared to be the opening of a mine shaft. Hanging precariously overhead was a weathered metal sign. Verde Valley Mining Company. Before Jake could fully appreciate the irony, his personal goon squad hauled him out of the van and kept him in step behind Agnes and Oliver by occasionally prodding him with the tips of their rifles. Inside the mine shaft, they boarded an elevator—a modern, well-lit elevator. So, this new Coalition compound was underground also, Jake realized, just like the one in Oregon directly beneath Redcom headquarters.

Once deep beneath the earth, they emerged into a

modern facility which had no doubt cost millions of dollars to build and equip. But as Agnes and Oliver led them down a long hallway, Jake didn't see more than two dozen people, which led him to believe that a vast part of their organization was still in Oregon. Did they intend to keep both secret bases active or did they plan to eventually phase out the one in Oregon?

Oliver opened a wide metal door, then stood back and waited for the guards to usher Jake inside before he and Agnes entered. The interior appeared to be an office of some sort, sparsely furnished, with tan walls and a gray concrete floor.

"You may all wait outside," Oliver told the guards. "If we need you, we'll call you."

As soon as the guards exited, Agnes turned to Jake. "Please sit down."

Jake pulled out a chair from a nearby metal desk and sat.

"For a man with a brilliant mind, you've made some very foolish mistakes," Agnes told him. "You should have gone directly to the FBI with the laptop. I'm sure that's what Dr. Brooks—or whatever her real name is—told you to do. You should have listened to her. But instead you tried to hack into our computer system and gave away your location. A very dumb thing to do. And we both know you aren't dumb."

"Dr. Brooks and I made a deal. I gave her the laptop and she allowed me to hand myself over to you. I wanted to be recaptured, which of course you've figured out.''

''As we speak, the access codes on our main computer system are being changed and will be changed at random to protect our files,'' Oliver said. ''The laptop will be useless to the FBI.''

''And there is no way the FBI can find us here,'' Agnes told Jake. ''We searched you for a homing device and found none attached to you and we disposed of your little microtransmitter, so you're quite alone here and totally at our mercy.''

Jake felt certain that if there had been any way to keep tabs on him from the motel to this underground compound, at this very minute Mariah knew where he was. The only thing she wouldn't know for sure was when to issue the order for the Feds to storm the compound. His only hope was that luck would be on their side and the federal agents would make their move at the right time.

''Are you bringing Gideon here?'' Jake asked.

''How sentimental and noble of you.'' Agnes walked up to Jake and smiled, her gaze locking with his. ''Even now, knowing that you've lost the war, that your life and Gideon's are in my hands, you're still arrogant and proud, aren't you? Enjoy feeling superior for the time being. All that will change soon enough.''

''Not unless you allow me to see my brother. Remember, you're the one who so wisely pointed out that Gideon is your only power over me.''

Agnes's smile vanished. She brought her face up close to his. "Do you believe you're invulnerable to torture?"

"Not invulnerable," he told her. "But I'll die before you break me. And I think you know that."

Agnes's facial muscles tightened. "Gideon is already here."

Jake almost reacted, but managed to remain totally in control.

Agnes frowned. "Would you like to see him?"

"You know that I would."

"I can arrange for him to be brought here, for the two of you to have some time alone together." She motioned to her husband. "Have them bring Gideon to me."

Oliver left immediately to do his wife's bidding. She turned back to Jake. "Now, I want something from you. A goodwill offer."

"What do you want?"

"I want to know Dr. Brooks's true identity."

"How should I know?"

"Is she a federal agent?"

"Probably."

"If you want to see Gideon, then you must give me something in return. I want information about Dr. Brooks. And it must be reliable information. If I later find out that you've lied to me..." She allowed her sentence to trail off, but the implication was plain.

"All I know is that she's not a Coalition psychiatrist, that she works for the government and her real name isn't Brooks. It's Mary Bailey. But other than what you already know, that's it.''

"Mary Bailey. You realize that I can check that name and find out something within a few hours.''

"She's a martial arts expert. And a crack shot.'' Jake paused for effect. ''And she told me that she killed Lester.''

Agnes huffed. ''You've told me very little, but it's enough…for now.''

She crossed the room, opened the door and left Jake alone. He took the opportunity to explore the small room. He searched for a bug of some type and within minutes found two. One in the empty staple gun on the desk and the other in the central ceiling light overhead. Before he could check further, he heard the door open. He hurriedly plopped his butt down on the side of the desk and crossed his arms over his chest.

Gideon walked into the room alone, unshackled and apparently not drugged. The door closed behind him, so Jake guessed that Agnes assumed the brothers might share vital information with each other if left alone. Looking at Gideon, he saw himself, so similar was their physical makeup. Same black hair. Same blue eyes. Identical height and weight within five pounds of each other.

Gideon came toward Jake, then the brothers grabbed each other and exchanged a hug. While hugging, Gideon whispered into Jake's ear. ''I got the disk and was able to send the information on it to

Gretchen and the others, then. I destroyed the disk, but they caught me before I could access the main computer.''

"I'm glad you're all right," Jake said loudly as they ended their brotherly embrace. Knowing that his siblings now possessed the info on the disk solved one problem, but left them with one far worse. They were both captives of the Coalition and if the FBI stormed the compound too soon, both he and Gideon could get caught in the crossfire.

"You look like you haven't been hurt too badly either," Gideon replied. "For a man who got himself caught by the Coalition. You did a dumb fool thing, brother."

"Talk about a dumb fool thing to do. Want to tell me how they got their hooks back into you?''

"Hell, Jake, I knew you'd never find the damn disk and would probably get yourself caught. What else could I do but come in after you?''

Jake chuckled. "What's that old saying? The road to hell is paved with good intentions.''

"Well, bro, we need to figure out a way to get out of this mess.''

Jake knew that his brother was as aware as he was that the room was bugged. He didn't kid himself that the two devices he'd found were the only two in the room. "Old Agnes and Oliver seem to have us by the short hairs, don't they?''

"Maybe we should just cooperate," Gideon said.

"Make it easy on ourselves. After all, they'll wind up reprogramming us eventually."

Jake put his arm around Gideon's shoulders and leaned close enough to whisper. "The Feds know where we are. They'll be storming this place soon." Jake cleared his throat.

"You don't have to remind me about Brooke." Gideon responded as if Jake had actually asked him something about his woman. "They've already reminded me that they can get to her quite easily and that they will if I don't help them."

Gideon's expression changed ever so slightly. Just enough to tell Jake that he understood help was on the way. Now all they had to do was play along with Agnes and do their damnedest not to get themselves killed before Mariah and her fellow agents rescued them. If they lived through this, Mariah would sure get a kick of saving his sorry hide once again.

The Coalition's Arizona compound was high in the Cerbat Mountains in the northwestern part of the state. At one time the region had been dotted with silver and gold mines. Although the area didn't look like much now, at one time millions of dollars of silver pay dirt had come out of the mountain. Many of the old horizontal shafts had been shut by dynamite, but undoubtedly the Coalition had bought property up here and constructed a compound in one of the old mines. The place was a safe haven undetectable by airplane surveillance and the entrance disguised as an abandoned mine kept it hidden from anyone who came upon the place by accident. The first thing Mariah had noticed was the rusty metal sign with the words Verde Valley Mining Company printed in bold letters.

"It's been four hours since they took Jake inside," Mariah said. "We know Gideon is already there, so Jake should have used the microtransmitter by now."

"Which leads us to believe they found the transmitter on him," Johnson said.

"We've waited long enough. If Jake could have gotten word to us somehow, he would have, so I say we strike now."

"I agree." Johnson took out his digital phone and dialed the number for headquarters. "All I need is an official okay."

Mariah waited while Johnson spoke softly into the phone. After hours of trailing the gray van, staying miles behind, and allowing the ever-changing parade of agents to keep closer tabs, they had waited for hours once they were in position to strike. Mariah's nerves were frayed. She kept wondering what was happening to Jake. Had they harmed him? Drugged him? Beaten him? Were they torturing Gideon Faulkner in front of Jake, trying to break him?"

"We're moving in," Johnson told her as he put his phone in his jacket pocket. "Jake Ingram's siblings have contacted the bureau with some very interesting information. It seems that someone—possibly Gideon Faulkner—was able to forward, via the

Coalition's own computer system, some very damaging information about the Coalition and their plans for future crimes. Within the hour other agents will be moving in on the Oregon compound."

"They know the location?" Johnson's assistant, Agent McBride asked, his black eyes wide with wonder.

"The coordinates for the location were included in the transmission to the siblings," Johnson replied.

Emotion tightened Mariah's chest and it was all she could do not to cry with joy. One of Jake's goals had been met. The Coalition was going down. If the information sent to Jake's siblings wasn't enough to put away every last member of the Coalition for life, then surely the bureau would find enough damaging info at the Oregon compound to accomplish the job. Now her only concern was Jake. And Gideon, of course, because his brother was Jake's top priority.

Mariah suited up. Full battle gear. Adrenaline pumped through her wildly. She was on an epinephrine high. Energy charged. Locked and loaded in every sense.

A surprise attack. Fast and furious. Take the enemy off-guard and destroy anything in the path of your objective. Despite the bureau's past mistakes, every man and woman prepared to storm the compound knew they were here to do a dirty job, one that might later either garner them some really bad press or win them the praise of a grateful nation. Either way, they were ready to do their duty.

Marksmen, trained as advance men, went in first, to prepare the way for the others. Once they sent back a signal to precede, Mariah and Johnson were in the first team to take the elevator and descend into the bowels of the earth. The minute the elevator opened, they heard gunplay. Using a defense mode, their team cautiously began moving into the open corridor. They took one room at a time, searching for Jake and Gideon. The advance team had done a great job of clearing the path, but as the minutes ticked by and they exposed one room after another, trekked up and down corridor after corridor, Mariah began to fear that Agnes and Oliver were holed up somewhere in this high-tech maze and had every intention of using Jake and Gideon as shields.

When they approached an unexplored hallway, one of the agents on the advance team hightailed it directly to Johnson.

"We've found them," the agent reported. "Grimble and Payne have asked to speak to the one in charge. They want to negotiate the terms of their releasing Ingram and Faulkner."

"Damn!" Just as Mariah had thought—Jake and Gideon remained hostages. The ever-clever Agnes would sacrifice anyone or anything to save her own neck. And Mariah knew that no way in hell was she going to trust the woman.

"You can't negotiate with her," Mariah told Johnson. "You can't trust her. You've got to know that."

"What do we do?" the advance guardsman asked.

"She's given us five minutes to get back to her with a reply. And my guess is that she's timing us down to the millisecond."

"Can you tell me anything about the room where she's holding Ingram and Faulkner?" Mariah asked.

"The best I can tell, all the rooms along this hallway are identical. Check out any one of them and it'll give you a good picture of the one where Payne and Grimble are holding their prisoners."

"Is there anyone else in the room, other than the four of them?" Johnson inquired.

"Yes, sir. We're pretty sure there are at least two others, but one of the guards is badly wounded and we're certain that Grimble took a hit to the shoulder."

Mariah turned to the agent. "Go back and tell her that Special Agent Johnson is in charge and he's on his way to talk to her."

"Mariah?" Johnson gave her a questioning stare.

"You talk to Agnes Payne. Stall her. I'm going to check out a couple of the rooms and see if I can find a way to get access to the room where Jake is. If I can find an alternate way in, then we have a chance of saving Jake and his brother, and maybe taking Agnes and Oliver alive. Keep radio communication open. I'll alert you about whatever I plan to do."

"That's good of you." Johnson mulled her suggestion over in his mind quickly, then said, "Be careful, will you, Daley. I would say don't take any unnecessary chances, but I know I'd be wasting my breath.''

Mariah grabbed the other agent's arm. "How many rooms down the hall is the room where Jake Ingram is being held?''

"The last one, ma'am. The sixth room on the right.''

Mariah turned to Johnson. "Wish me luck.''

"You'll need more than luck,'' he told her. "I'll pray for a miracle.''

While Johnson headed down the hallway with the other agent, Mariah scouted out two of the empty rooms—empty. She studied every aspect of the small rooms. The vent in the ceiling might be large enough for her to squeeze through—if she got rid of her coat, bulletproof vest and other equipment, then sucked in her breath and didn't mind the edges of the vent scraping her from shoulders to knees. After removing her heavy winter coat and vest, she shoved a desk directly under the vent, then placed a chair on top of the desk. She scrambled around in the desk drawers, searching for something she could use as a screwdriver. She found a letter opener and knew it was the closest thing she'd find to the tool she needed.

Using her communications device, Mariah contacted Johnson. "I'm going to crawl through the ventilation shaft. Once I'm inside, I figure I'll be making enough noise for them to hear me, so I'm going to need a loud distraction for a couple of minutes until I can make it from Room Two to Room Six.''

"On your signal, we'll provide the loud distraction," Johnson assured her.

Making sure the new weapon had provided her was secure in her new shoulder holster and checking the small flashlight stuffed inside her bra between her breasts, she climbed onto the table and then up onto the chair. Her fingertips just did reach the ceiling. Thank God she was five-ten and had long arms, otherwise she wouldn't have been able to use the letter opener to unscrew the bolts holding the vent cover in place. It took patience and tricky maneuvering to accomplish her goal, but eventually she managed to remove the cover. Instead of dropping it to the floor, which would have been the easiest solution, she climbed off the chair and laid the cover down on the desk. Maybe sounds weren't echoing down the hallway or the vent shaft, but on the off chance they were, she didn't want to alert the enemy about her plan.

After climbing back up onto the chair, she stood on her tiptoes, grabbed hold of the side of the gap in the ceiling and did the equivalent of a chin-press to hoist herself up and into the vent. Once inside, she scooted away from the opening. After undoing the first few buttons on her shirt, she pulled the flashlight out of her bra and turned it on. She shined the light forward and backward. The ventilation shaft was barely wide enough for a slender person. Most men would have a difficult time squeezing through the space.

She contacted Johnson again. "Get ready to make a very loud noise and keep it up for several minutes."

"Will do."

On her belly, using her arms and legs to advance her body along the ventilation tube, Mariah crawled as quickly as possible, heading directly to the final room on the right. Suddenly she heard voices shouting, then the *rat-a-tat-tat* of machine-gun fire. Good God, what was Johnson doing? What difference does it make as long as it distracts Agnes and her cohorts? While Mariah made her way down the shaft, the racket continued, effectively drowning out the rumbling sound of her body hitting against the sides of the air duct.

Hovering directly over the vent into Room Six, Mariah peered through the open slats. One guard lay either dead or unconscious in the far left corner. The other guard stood with his back to the wall near the door, his rifle up against his chest, a terrified look on his face.

Scanning the room further, she caught a glimpse of Oliver seated on the floor, his hands pressed tightly against his shoulder, blood oozing out between his fingers. He was wounded, but didn't look as if he was at death's door. Moving her gaze toward the opposite side of the room, she saw Jake standing tall and straight, Gideon at his side. Agnes Payne held a handgun to Gideon's head. Damn the woman.

She knew exactly how to keep both brothers in line without assistance from anyone else.

The gunplay outside the room tapered off. Johnson's voice called out loudly. "We just finished off what was left of your little army inside the compound."

"What do I care?" Agnes shouted. "The odds are still in my favor. I have Gideon and Jake. If you want them alive, then you'll agree to my terms."

"And what are your terms?" Johnson asked.

"Safe passage out of this place for my husband and me. I'll take Gideon with us until we're out of the country, then I'll set him free."

"What guarantee do I have that you'll keep your word?"

While Johnson and Agnes went back and forth on the details of a deal that would never happen, Mariah used her fingertips and the letter opener to loosen the screws in the vent cover from the back side. No easy feat. When she had two screws very loose, barely hanging on, she took a deep breath, then shoved the cover down, giving herself free access to a clear shot. The simultaneous events occurred at lightning speed. Mariah's first bullet hit Agnes in the head. She'd had no choice but to kill Agnes; otherwise the woman would have murdered Gideon. Jake swung forward and knocked the gun out of Agnes's hand just before she fell to the floor. The guard by the door realized what had happened and turned his rifle on Mariah. Jake bolted across the room and dove toward the

guard, knocking him to the floor. His rifle fired as he
hit the concrete, but the bullet missed Mariah, em-
bedding itself in the ceiling several feet away from
the vent. Gideon Faulkner noticed Oliver Grimble
removing a pistol from his pocket and called out to
Jake, who was closer to Oliver than Gideon was.
Mariah jumped down through the vent opening and
landed haphazardly. She fell on her side. Pain radiated through her hip. She rolled over twice, aimed
her gun and fired at the guard who had roused and
was aiming the rifle at Jake's back. Jake jumped on
Oliver, struggling with him for possession of the gun.
Mariah got to her feet and rushed over to Gideon
who stood watching while his brother and Grimble
tumbled about on the floor. Before Mariah could act,
the gun in Grimble's hand went off while it was
lodged between him and Jake. Mariah held her
breath. Please, God, please!

Jake rolled Grimble over and looked up at Mariah.
She almost cried when she saw the huge blood stain
across Jake's stomach.

"I'm all right," he told her as he came to his feet
a bit unsteadily. "It's his blood."

Mariah rushed toward Jake, then stopped abruptly,
common sense taking charge momentarily. "Johnson, it's all clear in here. What about out there?"

"All clear. We're already rounding up people and
taking them out of here. Does anybody in there need
medical attention?"

She looked at Jake. He shook his head and glanced

at Gideon, who said, "I'm fine." She went from body to body checking for vital signs. Agnes was dead, as Mariah knew she would be. The guard she'd shot was unconscious, but still alive, as was the other wounded guard. Oliver Grimble's pulse was weak and the gunshot had blown a good size hole in his belly. She didn't think he'd make it.

"One dead, three still alive," Mariah called out, then turned back to Jake. "You almost got yourself killed, you know."

"Nah, I wasn't worried." He reached out and pulled her into his arms. "I knew you'd show up at the last minute and rescue me."

Mariah threw her arms around his neck and plastered herself against him, uncaring that Oliver Grimble's blood covering the front of Jake's shirt rubbed off on her. "Well, from now on, you'd just better stay out of trouble. I can't spend the rest of my life rescuing you."

"Of course not. You're going to be too busy running the bureau and raising a couple of kids. If I'm lucky, they'll be a couple of kick-ass little girls just like their mother."

"Jake?" Her heart went wild. Her tummy fluttered.

"So, are you going to introduce me to the lady?" Gideon asked.

Jake kissed Mariah first, then turned her to face his brother. "This is FBI Special Agent Mariah Daley and the woman I intend to marry."

"What?" Mariah and Gideon said simultaneously.

"How about we get out of here?" Jake said. "I'd like to see the light of day again."

"Jake Ingram, don't you dare change the subject. You're talking about getting married and having kick-ass daughters and you haven't even asked me if I want to marry you or—"

Jake practically dragged Mariah out of the room, Gideon following them. And when they were in the hallway, which was now alive with activity, agents and medics all over the place, he kissed Mariah again. He kept kissing her and kissing her until he took her breath away.

When they came up for air, he grinned. "Mariah, I love you. Will you marry me?"

She swallowed several times, then cleared her throat. "Are you sure that's not gratitude talking? Or maybe you're on an adrenaline high or—"

"Or maybe I'm just plain crazy in love with you."

"Yeah, then there's that." She smiled at him.

"Well?"

"Yes, dammit, of course I'll marry you."

"Name the date. And make it soon. I don't want a long engagement."

Johnson issued orders to take Jake and Gideon out of the compound and have the medics topside check them over to make double sure they were all right. Mariah clung to Jake on the elevator ride to the surface and thought about a wedding date. As soon as they stepped out on firm ground, Gideon made a request.

"I'd like to call Brooke."

Spying Agent McBride out of the corner of her eye, Mariah called to him. "Get Mr. Faulkner a digital phone. He needs to let someone know he's safe and sound."

Jake pulled Mariah aside. "Gideon found the disk and he sent out the info on it to all our siblings, so—"

"We know. About the same time we stormed this place, another unit of federal agents were descending on the Oregon compound located under Redcom," Mariah said. "We're rounding up everyone involved with the Coalition. The new Code Proteus experiments will be confiscated. And even Rebelia, General DeBruzkya's domain, is on the run from American retaliation. Unfortunately, despite knowing that Bruno DeBruzkya hooked up with Croft and helped finance the New Code Proteus, we don't have enough hard evidence against him. The man is a megalomaniac and sooner or later, we'll get him. But except for the general, most of the loose ends concerning the Coalition should be tied up in a few weeks."

"It's difficult to believe that the Coalition is actually being destroyed, that what had become the main objective, my main goal in life this past year, has actually been achieved."

"And the new Code Proteus project has been

aborted. What happened with you and your brothers and sisters won't happen again.''

''I plan to make sure that it doesn't.''

''Jake?''

''Hmm?''

''March the twentieth.''

''What?''

She grunted, then poked him in the ribs. ''It's the first day of spring, Jake. It's a day of new beginnings, new hopes and dreams.''

''And the weather should be wonderful on Brunhia in late March.''

''Brunhia?''

''It's an island, just off the southern tip of Portugal, west of the Gulf of Cadiz.''

''I know where Brunhia is,'' she told him.

''It's been a safe haven for my family. I'd like for us to get married there, with only your immediate family and mine and our closest friends in attendance.''

''Sounds like an expensive undertaking,'' Mariah said. ''Even if we pool our resources, I don't think my folks and I can afford it.''

Jake nuzzled her nose with his, then reminded her, ''Aren't you forgetting that I'm a multimillionaire? I can easily afford to give you the wedding of your dreams.''

''I honestly hadn't given your financial status any thought.'' She snuggled to his side, allowing herself the luxury of being an eager, excited bride-to-be.

"By the way, the only thing I need in order to have the wedding of my dreams is the perfect bridegroom."

"Got anybody in mind?"

She punched him playfully. "As a matter of fact, I do. He's a genius. He's incredibly handsome and has a to-die-for body. And he's great in the sack."

"How great in the sack?" Jake asked jokingly.

"Well, if I had to describe his sexual prowess in one word—" she smiled at him, knowing that all the love in her heart was reflected in her expression "—that word would be superhero."

Jake burst into laughter, then lifted Mariah off her feet and swung her around and around before stopping and sliding her down his body until she stood there in his arms, her lips pressed against his. Oblivious to everything except each other, they celebrated being alive and in love. And destined for a long and happy future.

Epilogue

Isolated and rustic, the island of Brunhia came alive with nature's beauty in early spring. The locals had been hired to assist the outside staff which had been flown in to prepare for Jake and Mariah's wedding. In the beginning, Mariah had agreed for Jake to hire a wedding consultant, but when she'd fired three within the first two weeks, Jake had suggested that she simply tell him what she wanted and he'd hire people to give her exactly what she asked for—down to the last detail. So, today's affair would be simple, elegant and very private. Since there was only one safe water entrance to the island, which was adequately guarded, and the landing strip for small aircraft was also manned by locals hired by Jake's family, there would be absolutely no press at their wedding.

A week after the Coalition had crumbled and all the head honchos still alive were sitting behind bars, Jake had taken Mariah shopping for an engagement ring. She'd been shown one large diamond ring after another, but nothing had truly appealed to her. Oh, they'd all been breathtaking, outrageously expensive and what any woman in her right mind would want—

any woman except Mariah. In the end she'd asked Jake if he minded terribly if she didn't have an engagement ring, that all she really wanted was a wide gold band. He'd laughed and said, "Leave it to me to fall in love with a woman who could care less about money and all the fancy trappings that go with it."

They had come to the island ten days ago and enjoyed some time alone, just the two of them at the rustically elegant home owned by Gretchen's husband Kurt. Then Jake's entire family had arrived six days ago, including his adoptive brother Zack and his wife Maisy, as well as his parents. And his biological siblings and their mates had joined them for a real family reunion. Gideon and Brooke. Gretchen and Kurt. Marcus and Samantha. Faith and Luke. Connor and Alyssa.

Mariah had encouraged him to spend time with his brothers and sisters, for the six children to interact personally as siblings. They'd tossed around a football on the vast lawns, the brothers wrestling goodnaturedly and arguing over plays and the final score. They'd sat around in the evenings, listening to music, talking about everything and anything, while they munched on snacks and beer. And a couple of times, over in the wee hours of the morning, those still awake would reminisce about their childhood, about what each of them actually remembered. Gretchen and Faith had cried when they talked about Violet and Henry, and God knew that Jake—and he suspected his brothers, too—had felt like crying. They had lost so much—not only their parents, but a lifetime of growing up together. But they'd pledged that from here on out, nothing would ever keep them apart again.

Emotion lodged in Jake's throat as he thought about the strong bond he and his siblings had already forged. And he knew that in the future that bond of love and devotion would grow even stronger and be shared by their mates and their children.

While sharing good times, at long last, they had discussed their individual plans for the immediate future and everyone seemed to know their chosen path. Everyone except Gideon. Then Marcus had mentioned that his uncle, Russ Evans, down in Emerald Cove, Florida, owned a yacht company, but was also working on a top-secret submarine prototype for the U.S. Navy. Marcus had suggested that Russ could use Gideon's expertise on the project, and Jake wholeheartedly agreed. So, it appeared that the future looked pretty bright for all the Bloomfield kids.

This event had been the first time the entire family had been together since the Coalition had been destroyed and hundreds arrested, so they'd taken the opportunity to discuss what to do with their biological father's notes on genetic engineering. They had discussed the fate of Henry Bloomfield's legacy and in the end chose the lesser evil. Although they'd felt turning over the research material to anyone outside the immediate family was a risk, they had made a unanimous decision to hand over their father's research notes to the United States government. They sincerely hoped the information would be used only to benefit mankind and never again fall into the wrong hands.

Mariah's family, along with Jake's closest friends and hers, had come to the island three days ago—in time for the rehearsal dinner and the extravagant family bridal showers. While she and the other females had aahed and oohed over silver serving trays and silky negligees, Jake and the other men had indulged in a bachelor party extraordinaire. Although he hadn't been allowed to see Mariah today before the ceremony because she'd been fiercely guarded by her mother and her two matrons of honor, they had spoken on the phone. She had kidded him about just how wild the party had probably been last night, telling him she knew all about the fact that he, Matt, Eric and Ethan were once known as the Blues Brothers back in their days at the University of Chicago—because they broke so many hearts. But Jake had assured her that he'd been on his best behavior last night.

"From this day forward, there will be only one woman in my life and in my heart," he'd told her, then chuckled when he realized just how sappy his confession had sounded.

Mariah's matrons of honor—Jake's two sisters Gretchen and Faith—buzzed around her as her mother helped her straighten her bridal veil. Gretchen was mother to an infant daughter and her husband Kurt was a doting husband and father. Of course Gretchen wasn't the only mother among their friends and family, although she was the only one who had already given birth. Honey Evans Strong and her husband Max were expecting their first child as were Carey and Matt Tynan, and Gideon and Brooke.

Mariah's mom gave her a hug and a kiss before taking Mariah's grandmother's gold locket from its velvet case. "Something old and something borrowed." Sarah Daley placed the delicate chain around her daughter's neck. "And someday your daughter will wear this locket on her wedding day, just as I and my mother before me did."

Mariah and Jake wanted children, but had decided to wait a year before making plans for parenthood. She had a feeling that this locket just might be worn by more than one of her daughters. If Jake got his way, they'd have at least two kick-ass girls.

A few minutes later, with her arm laced through her father's, Mariah marched down the flower-strewn garden path that led her straight to the altar and the man she loved. Overhead the azure blue sky created a canopy more grand than the ceiling of any cathedral. This was Mariah's dream—an outdoor springtime wedding, with flowers everywhere and green grass and birds chirping. And Jake Ingram all decked out in a tuxedo.

The ceremony went by in a blur and Mariah found herself crying by the time she said "I do." Of course, she shed tears of happiness. And when Jake kissed her, she never wanted the moment to end. This was life at its best, a perfect moment out of time, blessed with complete joy.

After the minister introduced them as Mr. and Mrs. Jake Ingram, they raced down the grassy aisle toward the first huge pavilion set up for the reception. Jake pulled her aside and into his arms.

"Want to know where we're spending our honeymoon?" he asked, a devilish grin on his face.

"Oh, Jake, please tell me it's not Paris or Hawaii or—"

He kissed her to silence her, then said, "How does a very private cottage outside the fishing village near the cove sound to you, Mrs. Ingram?"

"Oh, Jake, you're not kidding, are you?"

Using his index finger, he drew an X across his chest. "Honest to goodness and hope to die if I'm not telling the truth."

"I can't think of anything more romantic than a tiny cottage overlooking the sea and just the two of us alone for a whole week."

"Make that two weeks."

"Oh, Jake you're so good to me."

"Sweetheart, that's easy to do when all you seem to want is me."

"You got that damn straight, mister! You're all I want. All I'll ever want."

They both laughed; and before their families and guests bombarded the pavilions, they hurried to cut their wedding cake.

Two months later, sometime shortly after seven in the evening on a rainy Thursday, a government official in Washington D.C. sealed Henry Bloomfield's notes on genetic engineering into a large expandable file folder, identical to others used by various government agencies. He buzzed for his assistant who entered his office.

"You know what to do with these," he told her.

"Yes, sir."

"I'll lock up," he said. "After you've delivered the package, go on home and spend time with your family. And tell your husband I apologize for having kept you so late."

"Yes, sir, thank you. And I don't mind staying late once in a while."

The young assistant, the wife of a D.C. policeman and the mother of twin toddlers, gathered up her purse and sweater in one hand and carried the large file folder in the other, then she walked out of the office and headed for the elevators. She punched the Down button and within minutes, alone in the elevator, she hummed a familiar tune as she descended to the building's basement. She marched down a long, narrow corridor, unlocked a door to the left and entered a massive room filled with row after row of filing cabinets. She searched the rows, looking for the "B" cabinets. When she finally found them, she had to use a step-stool to reach the highest cabinet. Efficient to a fault, she made sure the file was placed correctly in alphabetical order. Bloomfield. She wondered just who or what Bloomfield was. Of course, it didn't really matter. If the file had been of any importance at all, her boss wouldn't have had her bring it down here. These were the old, worthless files, of no interest to anyone.

Five extraordinary siblings.

One dangerous past.

Unlimited potential.

If you missed the first riveting stories from Family Secrets, here's a chance to order your copies today!

0-373-61368-7 ENEMY MIND by Maggie Shayne	___ $4.99 U.S.	___ $5.99 CAN.
0-373-61369-5 PYRAMID OF LIES by Anne Marie Winston	___ $4.99 U.S.	___ $5.99 CAN.
0-373-61370-9 THE PLAYER by Evelyn Vaughn	___ $4.99 U.S.	___ $5.99 CAN.
0-373-61371-7 THE BLUEWATER AFFAIR by Cindy Gerard	___ $4.99 U.S.	___ $5.99 CAN.
0-373-61372-5 HER BEAUTIFUL ASSASSIN by Virginia Kantra	___ $4.99 U.S.	___ $5.99 CAN.
0-373-61373-3 A VERDICT OF LOVE by Jenna Mills	___ $4.99 U.S.	___ $5.99 CAN.
0-373-61374-1 THE BILLIONAIRE DRIFTER by Beverly Bird	___ $4.99 U.S.	___ $5.99 CAN.
0-373-61375-X FEVER by Linda Winstead Jones	___ $4.99 U.S.	___ $5.99 CAN.
0-373-61376-8 BLIND ATTRACTION by Myrna Mackenzie	___ $4.99 U.S.	___ $5.99 CAN.
0-373-61377-6 THE PARKER PROJECT by Joan Elliott Pickart	___ $4.99 U.S.	___ $5.99 CAN.
0-373-61378-4 THE INSIDER by Ingrid Weaver	___ $4.99 U.S.	___ $5.99 CAN.
0-373-61379-2 CHECK MATE by Beverly Barton	___ $4.99 U.S.	___ $5.99 CAN.

(limited quantities available)

TOTAL AMOUNT	$_____
POSTAGE & HANDLING	$_____
($1.00 for one book; 50¢ for each additional)	
APPLICABLE TAXES*	$_____
TOTAL PAYABLE	$_____

(Check or money order—please do not send cash)

To order, complete the form and send it, along with a check or money order for the total above, payable to **Family Secrets,** to:
In the U.S.: 3010 Walden Avenue, P.O. Box 9077, Buffalo, NY 14269-9077;
In Canada: P.O. Box 636, Fort Erie, Ontario L2A 5X3

Name:_____

Address:_____ City:_____

State/Prov.:_____ Zip/Postal Code:_____

Account # (if applicable):_____

075 CSAS

*New York residents remit applicable sales taxes.
*Canadian residents remit applicable GST and provincial taxes.

Visit us at www.silhouettefamilysecrets.com   FSBACK11

Coming in May 2004

MOTHER BY DESIGN

by three *USA TODAY* bestselling authors

SUSAN MALLERY

CHRISTINE RIMMER

LAURIE PAIGE

Three best friends take fate into their own hands when they decide to become mothers. But their friendships are strained when dark secrets come to the surface. Can they heal their relationships— and even find love—before their due dates?

LOGAN'S LEGACY

Because birthright has its privileges and family ties run deep.

Available at your favorite retail outlet.

Where love comes alive™

Forrester Square

LEGACIES . LIES . LOVE .

The mystery and excitement
continues in May 2004 with…

COME FLY WITH ME
by

JILL SHALVIS

Longing for a child of
her own, single day-care
owner Katherine Kinard
decides to visit a sperm
bank. But fate intervenes
en route when she meets
Alaskan pilot Nick Spencer.
He quickly offers marriage
and a ready-made family…
but what about love?

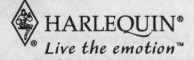

HARLEQUIN®
Live the emotion™

Visit the Forrester Square web site
at www.forrestersquare.com

FSQCFWM

"Joanna Wayne weaves together a romance and suspense
with pulse-pounding results!"
—*New York Times* bestselling author Tess Gerritsen

National bestselling author

JOANNA WAYNE

Alligator Moon

Determined to find his brother's killer, John Robicheaux finds
himself entangled with investigative reporter Callie Havelin.
Together they must shadow the sinister killer slithering in the
murky waters—before they are consumed by the darkness....

A riveting tale that shouldn't be missed!

Coming in June 2004.

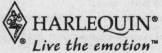

HARLEQUIN®
Live the emotion™

Visit us at www.eHarlequin.com

PHAM

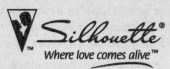

Silhouette®
Where love comes alive™

FAMILY SECRETS

Five extraordinary siblings.
One dangerous past.
Unlimited potential.

Collect four (4) original proofs of purchase from the back pages of four (4) Family Secrets titles and receive a specialty themed free gift valued at over $20.00 U.S.!

Just complete the order form and send it, along with four (4) proofs of purchase from four (4) different Family Secrets titles to: Family Secrets, P.O. Box 9047, Buffalo, NY 14269-9047, or P.O. Box 613, Fort Erie, Ontario L2A 5X3.

Name (PLEASE PRINT)

Address   Apt. #

City   State/Prov.   Zip/Postal Code

Please specify which themed gift package(s) you would like to receive:

❏ PASSION DT5N
❏ HOME AND FAMILY DT5P
❏ TENDER AND LIGHTHEARTED DT5Q

❏ Have you enclosed your proofs of purchase?

FAMILY SECRETS

One Proof
Of Purchase
FSPOP12R

Remember—for each package selected, you must send four (4) original proofs of purchase. To receive all three (3) gifts, just send in twelve (12) proofs of purchase, one from each of the 12 Family Secrets titles.

Please allow 4-6 weeks for delivery. Shipping and handling included. Offer good only while quantities last. Offer available in Canada and the U.S. only. Request should be received no later than July 31, 2004. Each proof of purchase should be cut out of the back page ad featuring this offer.

Visit us at www.eHarlequin.com   FSPOP12R